SPY MASTER

TRAITOR'S GAME

Also By Jan Burchett and Sara Vogler

The *Spy Master* series
☐ First Blood

The *Sam Silver* series
☐ Skeleton Island
☐ The Ghost Ship
☐ Kidnapped
☐ The Deadly Trap
☐ Dragon Fire
☐ The Double-cross
☐ The Great Rescue
☐ The Treasure Map
☐ The Sea Monster
☐ Dead Man's Hand

TRAITOR'S GAME

JAN BURCHETT
& SARA VOGLER

Orion
Children's Books

ORION CHILDREN'S BOOKS

First published in Great Britain in 2016 by Hodder and Stoughton

1 3 5 7 9 10 8 6 4 2

A CIP catalogue record for this book
is available from the British Library.

ISBN 978 1 4440 1070 1

Typeset by Input Data Services Ltd, Bridgwater, Somerset

Printed in Great Britain by CPI Group UK

The paper and board used in this book are from well-managed forests
and other responsible sources.

MIX
Paper from
responsible sources
FSC® C104740

Orion Children's Books
An imprint of
Hachette Children's Group
Part of Hodder and Stoughton
Carmelite House
50 Victoria Embankment
London EC4Y 0DZ
An Hachette UK Company

www.hachette.co.uk
www.hachettechildrens.co.uk

For Mike Spence, with love,
Sara and Jan

1

'**B**y St George, you'll lose your head for that!'
The angry roar had us all dropping our quills in fright – and woke Mister Scrope from his doze, papers lying forgotten on his lap. Mark looked across the scribes' table at me.

'His Majesty's injured shoulder is still hurting him then,' he said, nervously running his hands through his mousy hair.

'And it sounds as if he's coming up the stairs to our office!' I said.

'Do you want to kill me, you oaf!' came the bellowing voice, much closer now. 'Let go of my arm. I demand that this letter be copied and I will take it to the scribes myself.'

'He *is* coming!' gulped Mark, frantically trying to tidy himself and the table at the same time.

We heard anxious attendants pleading with our monarch.

'Then do it!' shouted the King. 'I expect the letter before the hour is up.'

The angry cursing moved out of earshot. Our little office high in the gatehouse at Greenwich Palace was safe from a royal invasion – for the moment.

'You'd both be better off getting on with some work,' hissed Oswyn Drage, acting for all the world as if he was Chief Scribe and not Mister Scrope.

Mark went anxiously back to his copying. I held Weasel-face's sharp-nosed gaze for a few seconds before I returned to the long boring laundry list in front of me.

The office door was flung open, making us all jump again. But it was only Robert Aycliffe, with another young courtier I didn't know. Mister Scrope scrambled to his feet to greet the gentlemen.

'Good morning, Mister Aycliffe,' he said, snatching at his spilled papers before they fluttered into the fire. 'Good morning, Mister Shawe.'

Aycliffe gave us all a friendly nod.

I noted that the newcomer was almost as tall as him, with short dark hair and a neat beard like his. His clothes were equally fine and both wore gold rings on each hand. Brother Matthew, my godfather who brought me up in St Godric's Abbey, had always said I was nosy but now I was turning it to good account. I was training myself to observe and remember these little things. Sometimes the most trivial information could be important.

Not that a palace scribe needed particular powers of observation. Those skills were useful for my other job. The job I couldn't speak about.

As far as everyone else was concerned, I was simply one of Thomas Cromwell's scribes. But Master Cromwell, the King's most trusted minister, ran a secret network of spies – and he'd recruited me to join their number. He refused to call us spies but that's what we were. We worked to keep King and country safe.

Aycliffe was another of his agents, but of course we didn't acknowledge each other. To other eyes he was just a gentleman of the Court who was training to be a lawyer, and I was just a scribe. Though I had a hunch that His Majesty also knew something of my extra work.

'I bring no writs or wills for you today,' announced Aycliffe. 'Instead a letter that must be copied at once.' He gave a wry smile. 'As you might have heard, the King orders it.'

Oswyn shot to his feet before Mister Scrope could answer. 'I will see to it myself,' he said in his oiliest voice.

Aycliffe gave him a nod. 'And we have a challenge for your lads, Mister Scrope.'

Even Mark sat up straight at that.

'Don't keep them too long from their work,' said the

Chief Scribe. 'We've a mountain of papers here, aside from the King's letter.'

'Listen, boys,' said Aycliffe. His friend was chuckling by his side. 'We all know how His Majesty hurt his shoulder while hunting. And as he is normally an active man, the tedium of recuperation has put him into an exceedingly bad temper . . .'

'You do not need to tell us,' Mister Scrope put in. 'Shame on you and Mister Shawe for making fun of such a terrible event.'

'Francis and I would never make fun of the King!' declared Aycliffe.

That was true. No one did – unless they had a death wish.

'Quite the opposite,' said Francis Shawe. 'We have a plan that we hope will restore our sovereign lord to good humour.'

'It seems that King Henry is in such pain that even his fool cannot take his thoughts from his wound,' said Aycliffe.

'Lord bless us!' exclaimed Mark. 'If Will Somers cannot cheer the King then there's no hope.' He immediately looked embarrassed to have spoken up in front of courtiers.

'We don't believe that,' said Aycliffe. 'We're looking for someone who can make our monarch laugh.' He pulled out a purse and waved it at us. 'There are five silver sixpences in here for the person who can do it.'

'Which I will equal,' added Shawe. 'A whole crown's worth to whoever succeeds. And Master Cromwell will give them thanks. When we were in the Presence Chamber earlier you'd have thought it was Cromwell's fault that the King's horse stumbled and threw him.'

I could see Oswyn's eyes looking greedily at the purse that Aycliffe was tossing in his hand as they left. He wanted to win it. So did I. I'd never had any money. My uniform, food and a space on the floor came with my job. My first payday was more than eleven months away. It seemed as near to me as the moon. But more important than that, I wanted to keep proving my worth to Thomas Cromwell. He'd taken a leap of faith when he recruited an abbey foundling.

I was determined to win the bet.

2

As I listed the endless number of smalls that had graced the palace laundry tub, I began to think of ways to make the King laugh. I'd done it once before, but last time it had been an accident with pigeon pies. I'd need something better this time. Something guaranteed not to go wrong. When His Majesty was in this mood he was like a bear with a sore head and might turn on anyone who annoyed him. I racked my brains for a joke that would suit a monarch. I drifted into a daydream in which the King practically fell off his throne with laughter at my witty remarks, clever card tricks and comical capering.

'This letter must go to the King straight away.' The Chief Scribe's voice broke into my thoughts. 'Who will take it?'

I got to my feet. 'I'll go . . .' I began. The letter was

a perfect excuse to get to King Henry. I'd think of something as I went to find him.

But Oswyn sprang up at the same time. 'No, I am the one to take it,' he said, flinging back his chair and rushing over to Mister Scrope. 'I wrote it after all.'

The clock in the Inner Court came to my rescue. It struck twelve.

'But Oswyn,' I said helpfully, 'it will be lunchtime before you get back. You don't want to be late for a meal, do you?'

I took advantage of his hesitation, grabbed the letter and made for the door.

'That's very thoughtful of you, Jack,' said Mister Scrope.

Oswyn was glaring at me, his face a picture – if the artist had painted sour milk! He didn't dare contradict Mister Scrope – even when the foundling from the abbey had got the better of him.

'Oh dear,' whispered Mark, as I passed. 'Now *you* will be late for lunch. You might even be too late. It's very bad to miss meals.'

He didn't need to tell me that. My stomach would let me know soon enough.

'I heard of a boy who missed too many meals,' Mark went on, 'and he got so thin he fell down a rabbit hole.'

'I wouldn't want to share that fate,' I said solemnly. Mark was my friend and I wasn't going to mock his beliefs, no matter how farfetched. 'Perhaps you can save me something.'

Mark nodded earnestly. 'A sensible idea.'

I hurried down the gatehouse stairs to the first floor and past Master Cromwell's rooms. Greenwich Palace wasn't as huge and rambling as Whitehall, where I'd started my employment, but it was still big. Luckily for me my godfather, Brother Matthew, had trained my mind well and I'd memorised the way to the Presence Chamber. That was where the King would be. I was sure it wouldn't be the only time I'd need my memory skills. King Henry seemed to change palaces at a whim.

I reached the long gallery. I'd started practising a silly, lolloping walk I'd seen Will Somers do for the King, when I realised I wasn't alone. An old lady with white hair was coming up the stairs ahead. She took one look at me and her eyes grew wide with concern.

'Jack!' she yelped. 'You've got a shocking limp. What in the name of mercy have you done to yourself?'

Mrs Pennycod, the pastry cook, was a kind soul who looked out for my welfare. I'd first met her under the table in the kitchens at Whitehall. At least, I'd been under the table hiding from a yeoman guard and she'd slipped me a chicken leg. I think she took to me because I reminded her of her niece's boy who lived far away. She usually thought I was starving. I believe she thought I was dying now!

'I'm all right, Mrs Pennycod,' I began. 'I was just . . .'

'Come here, my little Jackanapes,' Mrs Pennycod interrupted. She grabbed my arm and made me sit down on the stairs. 'Let's have a look at that leg.'

I tried again. 'There's nothing wrong with it . . .'

'You don't have to act all brave in front of me,' tutted Mrs Pennycod. 'I know what you need.'

She rummaged in her apron pocket and produced a huge chunk of crumbling gooseberry pie. 'I've been carrying this around in case I saw you. You may be wounded, but I'll not have you starving.'

I took it gratefully. As soon as I'd finished I sprang to my feet.

'God in heaven, it's a miracle,' exclaimed Mrs Pennycod. 'You're cured!'

'Gooseberries have wonderful healing properties,' I said with a grin. 'And no one makes a pie as well as you.' I made her a bow. 'Now I must be off to entertain the King.'

'Going to win that bet?' said the old lady, beaming at me from under her cap. She reached up and pinched my cheek. 'If anyone can, then it'll be you, my Jackanapes.'

She bustled off. I decided that capering for His Majesty was best left to Will Somers.

I opened the door of the Presence Chamber. This was my first look inside. It was huge, with a high-vaulted ceiling and King Henry's arms depicted in the stained-glass windows. The three lions on his shields looked about as angry as the King himself since his accident. I slipped inside and closed the door behind me.

Hundreds of courtiers were squashed onto long benches, with servants scurrying backwards and forwards carrying platters of food. Mark had explained that everyone wanted to be close to their monarch. So when he moved palaces, they all swarmed off with him.

But they were unlucky today, and so was I. The King wasn't there. I should have realised. There were no yeomen guarding the door. Then I spotted Master Cromwell sitting at a table with a platter of food in front of him. I was surprised – he usually took lunch in his room while he worked. However, there he was, large as life in his fur-lined robes. If I knew anything about him, he wouldn't be there for a social chat. His companions were all talking, apart from a small, thin man who was writing intently on a piece of parchment. Cromwell wasn't joining in the chatter either. His hooded eyes were on his plate but I guessed his thoughts weren't on food. There must be a good reason why he was among the courtiers today. I'd warrant he was listening for some snippet of information dropped by a careless tongue. There must be something serious going on. Something secret that was threatening the King.

I was approaching him to ask where the King might be found when the doors of the Presence Chamber were flung open, nearly flattening a poor page against the wall. A maidservant ran in, making a beeline for a stout lady sitting nearby. She bowed briefly, her eyes wide with shock.

'Lady Gooldsbury,' she cried in alarm. 'Such villainy. You've been robbed.'

Her mistress let out a shrill scream and toppled backwards off her bench in a faint.

'Tend to Lady Gooldsbury,' commanded Cromwell and two servants ran forwards to do his bidding. The maidservant went to join them, but Cromwell beckoned to her. 'Tell me the whole,' he said calmly.

'It's her favourite French hood, sir,' began the servant, 'purloined from its stand.'

'Forgive me for suggesting it, but could it be lost and not stolen?' asked Cromwell. 'Your mistress does suffer from . . . absentmindedness.'

'That's true, sir,' agreed the woman. 'Only last week she had us searching for a pair of gloves she'd got in her hand all along, but this is different. It was there one moment and gone the next.'

'Strange indeed,' he said. 'Now go to her ladyship. I will sort the matter.'

'Thank you, sir,' said the servant and she ran to help the two young boys who were flapping napkins uselessly at Lady Gooldsbury. All the diners were gossiping loudly about the theft, except for the small thin man who was humming to himself and writing musical notes on his page.

I was just wondering how he was managing to concentrate when I realised my master was calling me over.

'Is that something I have to deal with?' he asked, indicating the letter in my hand.

I'd forgotten all about it in the uproar. 'No, sir,' I

said. 'It's a letter His Majesty wanted copying. Where can he be found?'

'Deliver it to his Privy Chambers.' I bowed and went to go but he stood and put a hand, heavy with rings, on my arm. 'Let me check it first, boy,' he said. 'Come.'

He took the letter over to the window as if to read it by the light. I followed. 'Well, Jack,' he said in a low voice, 'it seems a petty matter, the mislaying of a French hood.'

'Yes, sir,' I said. There was more to come, I was sure of it. He was going to involve me in whatever grave business had brought him to sit among the chattering courtiers. His next words dashed my hopes.

'But it is the sort of petty matter that could annoy the King and his temper does not need stirring at this time! The thief must be caught before His Majesty hears of it.'

'You wish me to investigate, sir?' I asked, trying not to sound too disappointed.

He nodded. 'Begin directly. You can tell Mister Scrope that I need you for a small errand.'

Oh well, I thought. *It beats copying out laundry lists.*

He tapped his ring on the nearest table. It was a tiny sound in all the hubbub but it worked. Everyone fell silent and turned to him – even the small, thin man.

'The King is to hear not one whit of this theft,' Cromwell announced. 'We do not wish to upset him any further.'

Everyone could see the wisdom in that. There was a frantic nodding of heads.

He turned back to me. 'I will take the King's letter to him.'

I handed it over and took my leave as a gaggle of servants tried to heave Lady Gooldsbury off the floor.

The other scribes were coming back from lunch when I got to our door. Mister Scrope sighed heavily when he heard my message from Cromwell.

'You must do as our master bids,' he said. 'Though there's much to be done here.'

He ambled into the office. I guessed that he was going to be very busy, sleeping off his lunch in front of the fire!

Mark nudged my arm and slipped some manchet bread from his sleeve into my hand.

'Thanks,' I whispered.

I turned to go and start my investigation. Oswyn stepped into my path.

'Running off, as usual?' he said coldly. 'What are you up to this time?'

'Working hard,' I replied. 'For our master.'

'Are you sure?' Oswyn looked at me with a faint smile. It held an unspoken threat. 'Master Cromwell has never bothered much with us scribes before. If I didn't know any better, I'd think there was something strange going on.'

3

My first instinct was to thump Oswyn Drage. That would make him forget about doing any 'thinking' for a while. But I stopped myself. Mark had warned me how Oswyn had managed to cause previous scribes to lose their jobs. Weasel-face had a younger brother and he wanted a position for him.

My scribing was the perfect cover for my secret work for Cromwell. If I lost one job I'd certainly lose the other. Anyway, I told myself, I had more important things to think about than his silly taunts, although my fist was itching to knock the stuffing out of him.

I'd begin my investigation by talking to Lady Gooldsbury's maid. I was sure to find her in her mistress's bedchamber. Lady Gooldsbury might be the size of the abbey sow, but I took a chance that the servants had managed to deliver her to her room by the time I got there.

I had no idea where that room was, so I decided to ask Mark. But I had to get the information without telling him about the theft.

'Master Cromwell has ordered me to enquire after Lady Gooldsbury's health,' I told him quietly.

Mark looked worried. 'What's wrong with her?'

'She fainted at lunch,' I told him. That was true.

'Do you think it was something in her food?' said Mark. 'Only I heard of someone who ate a maggot and passed out in his potage. He would have drowned if his friend hadn't rescued him.'

'I don't think it was the food,' I said, keeping a straight face. 'Master Cromwell wants to know how she is. Where's her chamber?'

'Go down one flight of stairs and turn left by the marble Adam and Eve. Follow that gallery, past the nymphs sitting on a bronze unicorn, then, when you get to the statue of Apollo with no arms, turn right. Lady Gooldsbury's room is the last one along that corridor.'

'Thank you,' I said. 'I'll be off then.'

'I haven't finished,' said Mark anxiously. 'If you turn the corner and go along the gallery that looks over the river and reach the big gold doors with yeomen barring your way – you've gone too far.' He gulped. 'That's the King's apartments, although I've never been along there so I can't tell you exactly where they are. It might not be the first door you come to, you see.'

'Don't worry . . .' I began.

15

'But I shall!' whispered Mark. 'It would be so easy to make a mistake.'

'I'll be very careful,' I assured him, and escaped.

There were servants in the corridor, scrubbing the floor, dusting the portraits of long dead kings and polishing the many statues. King Henry had surprised everyone with his sudden move to Greenwich and now the servants were trying to get it clean for him. I darted round them, munching my bread as I went.

Just as I'd got to a stone archer with a big nose, someone called my name.

'Jack!' Cat Thimblebee came hurrying towards me, carrying a basket of linen. Her red hair was escaping from under her cap and her eyes were sparkling with curiosity.

'What are you doing near the bedchambers?' she demanded. For a second I'd been pleased to see Cat – before she started sticking her nose into my business!

Before I could open my mouth to reply she put the basket down – on my foot – and folded her arms. 'I haven't seen you since we arrived. I've been that busy. You wouldn't credit how many courtiers need their clothes mending after one short trip from Whitehall to Greenwich. You'd think they'd rowed themselves down the Thames!' She looked about to make sure no one was in earshot. 'I expect you want to arrange another riding lesson. God knows you need it!'

I ignored the last comment. It was true that I wasn't exactly an expert horseman yet. The secret lessons Cat had given me at Whitehall were proving that there was a lot more to staying on a horse than I'd realised. In fact all I could do so far was bounce about helplessly in the saddle, getting a sore bum and being laughed at by my irritating instructor. The trouble was, I really needed to learn. Master Cromwell seemed to think I could already ride. This may have been because that's what I'd told him!

'When can I have another lesson then?' I asked.

'Hmmm,' said Cat, scratching her chin as if she was thinking hard. 'It's going to be difficult to fit you in. A skilled seamstress like me is given such a lot of mending to do.' She nodded towards her basket.

'If you're too busy I'll find someone else . . .' I began, calling her bluff.

'No need,' said Cat airily. 'Come to the park at dawn tomorrow. I'll meet you at the top of the hill behind the palace. We won't be seen.'

'Are you sure you'll be able to borrow a horse here at Greenwich?'

'Greenwich, Whitehall, Hampton Court, wherever we are I can always sneak one out of the stables when I want to. No one's caught me yet. And I'm doing them a favour. The horses need exercising.'

'Very well then,' I said. 'As long as it's not Diablo the devil stallion.'

'You'll get what you're given!' laughed Cat.

'Now I must go,' I said, shifting her basket off my foot.

But Cat stood in my way. 'Wait a minute,' she said, peering intently into my face. 'You're up to something, Jack Briars.'

'Well . . .' I began, wondering if she would ever let me get on.

'I knew it!' said Cat in delight. She lowered her voice as a servant walked by. 'You've got a special job to do, haven't you?'

I hesitated. I was supposed to keep my extra work for Master Cromwell a secret. And indeed I'd started off by not telling a soul, until somehow Cat had made herself my partner in my investigations.

I decided to let her in on my mission. I had to admit, though certainly not to her, that she'd been very useful in the past. But before I could open my mouth she'd started up again.

'It's about the theft!' she cried. 'Lady Gooldsbury's French hood!'

'Not so loud,' I hissed. 'The King mustn't know anything about it – and no one must know that I'm investigating. How did you hear of it?'

'Meg, that's her maidservant, found the hood had gone and went running out into the passage, screaming her head off,' said Cat. 'That's typical of her. She'd make a mountain out of a dung heap. Ned the log boy heard her as he was delivering kindling for the fires along here and he told Mister Sorrel in the kitchen and Mister Sorrel told me.'

I might have known. The servants' gossip machine was always well oiled.

'It must not come to the ears of the King,' I said. 'Make sure you pass that around. Master Cromwell's orders.'

'Very well.' Cat sniffed. 'It's not exactly life or death though, is it!'

I chose to ignore that stinging remark.

'Then you won't want to hear any more about it,' I answered with a shrug.

'I certainly do,' exclaimed Cat. 'You'll be sure to need my help. '

'Come with me,' I ordered, heading off down the corridor, determined to show her I was in charge. She scooped up her basket and trotted along beside me. 'Mister Cromwell wants it all sorted quickly.'

'Then it's lucky you found me,' said Cat. 'Four eyes are better than two.'

God's teeth, she always got the last word!

4

Cat seemed to know every servant we passed.

'That's Dickon,' she said, nodding to a man who was rubbing a tapestry with a hunk of bread.

'What's he doing?' I whispered.

'Cleaning it, of course.' Cat waved at a young boy scurrying by with a chamber pot. 'Didn't you clean the tapestries at the abbey?'

'We didn't have any,' I told her. 'At least, the abbot did in his private tower but any bread that went in there would have gone straight in his mouth, the greedy gorbelly.'

We passed Mark's nymphs sitting on their unicorn and turned the corner by the armless Apollo. I could see the door to Lady Gooldsbury's chamber now. A servant ran past us and hurried into the room before it.

'Hello, Cat,' he called over his shoulder.

'That's Isaac,' said Cat. 'I haven't seen him since we

were at Hampton Court for Christmas. I must have a chat with him.'

'Off you go then,' I replied. 'I've got more important things to do.'

'You're not getting rid of me that easily,' sniffed Cat. 'It'll wait.' She bustled up to Lady Gooldsbury's door and knocked before I could stop her.

Meg the maidservant appeared. She looked grumpy.

'My mistress is asleep,' she hissed. She didn't need to tell us. Fearsome snores were rumbling out of the room. 'Sir William Butts came with a calming draught, and him physician to the King no less, but she's like to wake at the slightest sound so go away!'

She went to close the door.

I opened my mouth to start pleading but Cat chipped in before I could.

'You can't send us away, Meg,' she said. 'Not without telling us what happened.' She put on a simpering smile. 'After all, you were the one who discovered the dreadful theft. You'll be really popular at supper – but me and Jack here can't wait till then . . . and you do tell such a good tale.'

Cat's wheedling worked. The maidservant's face lit up.

'The French hood was on a stand as it always is,' she told us eagerly. I think she was enjoying her sudden importance.

'Can you be sure?' I asked. Cromwell had said Lady Gooldsbury was very absentminded.

'Indeed I can,' retorted Meg. 'I'd been mending it. There was a seed pearl come loose and I hadn't any thread so I went off to find Sally who was just outside and sure to have some. I was only gone for a minute getting the cotton from her and I shut the door and when I went back in, the room was the same as I'd left it. Or so I thought. And then I saw it – or rather I didn't. The French hood . . .' She sucked in a breath. 'It was gone. Just think, I could have been inches away from the thief!'

'So he got in while you were chatting with Sally,' said Cat, as blunt as ever.

Meg looked highly offended. 'You take that back, Cat Thimblebee! Are you saying I'm blind? They'd have had to walk right past me and open the door – which they didn't. I don't let anyone near my mistress's room without my say-so.'

Cat opened her mouth to make a retort.

'No one would think it of you,' I assured Meg, elbowing Cat in the ribs to keep her quiet. 'But it is a mystery. Was the window open?'

'What and lose all the heat from the fire? I've had enough of your stupid questions. Stop wasting my time.' Looking daggers at Cat and me, Meg flounced inside and shut the door in our faces. But not before I'd caught a glimpse of a room crammed with furniture, each piece covered with silly ornaments.

'The thief must have got in this way,' said Cat, 'whatever *she* says. He certainly won't have come down the chimney while there was a fire blazing.'

'I wish I could have gone in and had a nose round,' I said.

'At her ladyship snoring like a pig?' said Cat.

'Don't be silly. The thief might have left a clue of some sort.'

'Like what?'

'I'll know it when I see it,' I said mysteriously. I wasn't going to tell Cat that I didn't have any idea what I'd be searching for.

Before I could think what to do, Isaac came bursting out of the next chamber.

'Help!' he yelled. 'There's been another theft!'

'What's been taken?' I asked quickly.

'It's Sir Basil's seal ring,' replied Isaac. 'The box was open. It was empty.'

'Could it just be lost?' said Cat.

'No,' said Isaac. 'It's always kept in that rosewood box by his bed and I know he didn't take it today. He only got up in time for luncheon so he had no need of it. But I can't stand here talking – I must tell my master.' He ran off down the corridor.

'Quick,' I said to Cat. 'Let's get inside. Before he comes back with Sir Basil.'

We slipped through the door. Cat plonked her basket down on Sir Basil's bed and warmed her hands in front of the fire. 'I've never been in here before. You could sleep about a hundred of us on that floor – and have room to turn over.'

I glanced quickly round the chamber. Sir Basil's riding boots were arranged in a neat line against the wall and there wasn't a single wrinkle in the velvet hangings round his bed. It was hard to believe the thief had been in here at all. There was no sign of a disturbance. Meg had said that Lady Gooldsbury's room seemed untouched too. I checked all the places where a robber could be hiding. The chamber was empty and the window tightly shut.

'This is strange,' said Cat, picking up a heavy gold chain encrusted with pearls and rubies. 'Why didn't the thief take this? It must be worth a lot more than a little ring.'

'I think you've hit on a clue, Cat,' I said. 'And what about French hoods? Would they be valuable?'

'Well any of them would be riches to me,' laughed Cat. 'But not to someone wealthy like her ladyship. I've seen hers. It was just a bit of velvet and some seed pearls.'

'It's not much to tell Master Cromwell,' I said thoughtfully. 'The theft of two objects of little value.'

Cat picked up her basket and we were about to leave when she caught my arm. 'Did you hear that noise?' she said in an awed whisper.

'I didn't hear a thing,' I replied.

'You must have. It was really close.'

'Isaac isn't coming back, is he?' I asked in sudden alarm. 'We can't be found in here.'

'No. It was inside this room. It was a sort of swishing noise. Then a low moan.'

Cat pulled me out of the room and slammed the door shut. I could see she was shaken.

'I'm not going in there again!' she told me, casting her eyes about nervously. 'I know exactly what that noise was. It was a ghost.'

5

Cat wasn't joking. I don't think I'd ever seen her look so scared.

'It was the ghost of Duke Humphrey,' she breathed, edging away from Sir Basil's door. 'I'm certain of it. The duke owned the palace many years ago – and I've heard tell how his throat was slit and his blood dripped down the walls and now his ghost walks the palace.'

'That's an excellent tale,' I said. 'But it doesn't exactly help us to find the thief.'

'Of course it does,' said Cat. 'No human thief would take things of such little value. It was Duke Humphrey himself. It all fits. A ghost isn't bothered by closed doors and windows.'

'Why would he want a seal ring and a French hood?' I demanded. 'He can't sell them, and he can't exactly wear them!'

'Don't question the doings of a phantom,' said Cat darkly.

A sudden cry had us spinning round. 'Hurry up!'

A servant was outside the next chamber, prodding the back of a carpenter who was frantically trying to prise open the door. 'Her ladyship will be here at any minute and she's sure to blame me for her door being stuck, even though it was her that slammed it when she went off in a temper this morning.'

'Sorry, Gwen,' puffed the carpenter. 'It's . . . the devil's own job to . . . release it.' As he spoke the wood splintered with a crack, the door flew open and he tumbled into the room.

'What is the meaning of this?' A battleship of a woman came storming along the corridor, nearly flattening Cat and me against the wall. A weedy little man trotted along in her wake.

'That's Lady Tresham,' Cat whispered, 'with her husband cowering behind her. Terrified of her, is Sir Rowland.'

'And so's the carpenter, by the looks of it,' I answered.

'The door was stuck, my lady,' quavered Gwen. 'It was . . .'

But Lady Tresham had stepped over the carpenter and stomped into the room. 'Never mind that. Come and help me change.'

Almost immediately she stormed out again. 'What have you done with my fan, Rowland?'

'Nothing, my love,' came the timid reply. 'Might you have . . . lost it?'

'Lost it?' Lady Tresham was so shrill that we almost staggered back from the blast. 'I left it on the bed.'

'Then it must still be there,' her poor husband tried to insist.

'Are you calling me a liar?'

'No, my love.'

'Then it has been stolen!'

'No one can have got in until this good man released the door . . .' Sir Rowland tailed off as his wife stormed back into their room.

Cat grabbed my arm. 'What did I tell you?' she muttered, her face pale. 'Duke Humphrey's at the bottom of this.'

'He can't be . . .' I began.

'Then you tell me how a living thief got in there,' she demanded. 'The door was jammed.'

I had to admit she was right. We'd all seen the force the carpenter had used to open it.

However, I had no intention of going back to my master and telling him a ghostly robber was at work in the palace! Surely there was another explanation. I had to see inside the chamber.

'Wait here,' I said. 'I'm going to solve this.'

Cat snorted in disbelief.

I approached Lady Tresham. 'Can I be of service, my lady?' I asked with a bow. 'I am one of Master Cromwell's scribes. He will wish to know about your loss. Allow me to report the details to him.'

Luckily Lady Tresham was too shocked to wonder why I'd suddenly popped up in her chamber. 'All he needs to know is that my favourite fan has been taken. I left it here on the bed.' She began to pace up and down the chamber, ignoring the carpenter who had managed to get to his feet and now stood patiently waiting for his pay.

I cast a quick glance around. A single closed window and a single door, the same as Sir Basil's chamber.

'Thank you, my lady,' I said, and bowed again. 'I shall report what has happened to my master. There have been other thefts.' Lady Tresham gave a shriek at that. 'But His Majesty must not know of them. Those are Master Cromwell's orders.'

I joined Cat in the corridor. 'I can't see how anyone could have got into these rooms,' I told her. 'I need to have a proper look round.'

'No you don't,' she declared. 'It was definitely a ghost – the ghost of Duke Humphrey!' Now that she'd decided she'd been right all along, her fear was mixed with glee. Her triumphant voice rang down the passage.

Unfortunately it reached the ears of Lady Tresham. 'Duke Humphrey?' we heard her screech. 'The one whose head was chopped off and rolled around on the floor howling about how he'd have his revenge?'

'I'm sure it's not . . .' her husband began.

'Save your breath, man!' shrilled Lady Tresham. 'I will not stay another night in this chamber!'

'But, my love, there are no other chambers free in the palace,' said Sir Rowland. 'We were very lucky to be housed in this one . . .'

'Then we shall take lodgings in Greenwich Village!' declared her ladyship. She burst out of the room, swept past us and made off down the passage. Her husband, maidservant and the carpenter, still wanting his pay, trotted after her. Sir Rowland was bleating at her to reconsider. That seemed a forlorn hope.

'You've really caused a stir!' I told Cat.

'I've done you a favour as well,' she retorted.

'How?'

'The room's empty,' said Cat smugly, 'so you can have your proper look round now.'

I said nothing. I never understood how Cat always got the better of me in any argument.

'But I don't advise it,' Cat went on. 'That ghost could pop out at any minute.'

'Then I'll go on my own,' I told her, flinging the door open.

Cat immediately scuttled in after me, dropping her basket on the floor. Curiosity had obviously got the better of her fear. 'What are you looking for exactly?' she asked.

'I've got to find out how the thief got into these rooms,' I said. 'We know he didn't use the doors, and the windows were shut.'

'So how can he have got in here unless he was supernatural . . . ?' Cat stopped, scaring herself all over again.

'There's one more possibility,' I said quickly, going to the window. 'He could have climbed up here from the courtyard. He could have entered each room this way.'

'But how?' argued Cat. 'Like you said, all the windows were shut.'

'He might have a really clever way of getting in from the outside.'

She gave me a look. 'You're going to try it, aren't you?' she said. 'Not content with climbing over Whitehall Palace, you're now going to have a go at Greenwich.'

'That was different,' I told her. 'I was escaping from the guards then.'

Cat picked up her basket. 'I'd love to stay and watch but I'd better get on with this mending or Mr Wiltshire will have my hide.'

'I'll let you know what I find out.'

'Good,' she said over her shoulder as she left the room. 'For I'll be all agog until you do. And you'll be sure to need my help again.'

She'd gone before I could answer her back – annoying wretch!

I found the nearest staircase and was soon out in the Inner Court. The courtyard was bounded on all sides by the old red brick palace. No one was about, which

31

was unusual, but it had started to rain and sensible folk were keeping inside.

The chambers where the thefts had occurred were on the west wall. I looked up at the three windows, blinking the raindrops out of my eyes. The brickwork was smooth with no helpful footholds. However, ivy grew almost to the windows. The stems were thick and strong and seemed well rooted to the stone. It was as good as a ladder to a thief. Above the windows, the roof was steep. It was unlikely that anyone could get down that way.

Something about the three windows seemed different from the others on the same floor but I didn't have time to ponder on it. I had to carry out my test before anyone came along.

Lady Tresham's empty chamber was the third along from the corner. That was the one to aim for. I doubted that Sir Basil or Lady Gooldsbury would take kindly to me gawping in at them.

No one was in sight so I began to climb.

I pulled myself up, past the rooms on the ground floor. But the ivy that had looked so close to the window from below stopped well short of it. I'd need arms as long as oars to reach the sill. Even the tallest of thieves couldn't have got into the rooms this way.

'Hey!' came a shout below me. 'What do you think you're up to?'

6

I nearly fell off the ivy!

Robert Aycliffe was standing below, a huge grin on his face.

'I might have known it would be you, Jack,' he called as I clung to the stems. 'What are you doing scrambling all over the palace?'

Footsteps rang out over the paved stones. A couple of yeomen guard were crossing the courtyard. My heart sank as they came to investigate.

'I'm . . . retrieving my cap,' I called. 'The wind blew it up here. I shall be in terrible trouble from Mister Scrope if I lose it.' I pretended to sound very anxious at the thought.

'But your cap is on your head,' said Aycliffe.

Curse the man! He was enjoying this. Well, he wasn't going to get the better of me! And it was good training for a spy – finding ways to wriggle out of tricky situations.

'I've just this minute rescued it,' I said.

I clambered down and jumped the last few feet onto the flagstones, pleased with my ready excuse. The guards laughed and went off.

'You're still a resourceful play actor, I see. I haven't forgotten how you turned into a crookback pig herder and completely fooled me. However, you forgot one thing.'

'What?' I asked.

'Your cap can't have blown up onto the ivy,' he laughed. 'There's no wind today!'

I hadn't exactly wriggled out of that tricky situation!

He smiled, enjoying my discomfort. 'So what were you really doing?'

The yeomen had gone out of earshot now. I knew I could trust Aycliffe. 'I'm investigating the thefts for Master Cromwell,' I told him. 'I was checking whether the thief could have got in through a window. It's a puzzle and I mean to solve it. But I bet you're dealing with something more important than missing French hoods and fans.'

A dark cloud seemed to pass briefly over Aycliffe's face. 'Stick to finding your thief, Jack. Especially at the moment.'

I looked at him. There was a warning in his eyes. And I knew in that instant that I was right. Something much bigger and more secret than petty theft was going on. Now I had no doubt that was why Cromwell had taken lunch with the Court.

'I'm always at your service,' I said. 'If there's anything you need my help with . . .' I knew he would understand what I meant.

'You have many talents,' replied Aycliffe, 'and you'll be called upon to use them again one day.' His tone suddenly hardened and for a moment he looked almost threatening. 'But for now, keep your nose out.' The smile was back as if nothing had happened. 'After all, you're protecting the King from irksome worry. And that means protecting us all from his temper!'

He strode away.

I'd have given anything to know what was going on. But instead I'd been warned off.

The rainwater was dripping down my neck now. I took one last look up at the rooms where the thefts had occurred. And then I realised that my eyes had not tricked me earlier. There *was* something odd about the three windows. All the others on that floor were larger and set lower in the wall. I couldn't think how this was relevant to my investigation but I was pleased to have solved what had been niggling away at my brain.

I paced the flagstones, glaring at the walls of the courtyard as if the answer was going to appear in big letters on the brickwork. Was I missing something obvious? The windows and roof were inaccessible and, by all accounts, the thief hadn't used the doors. And I was certain that there wasn't a supernatural force at work, despite what Cat said. Well, reasonably certain.

I couldn't stay away from my scribing any longer. I'd have to go and do some work and see if any bright ideas popped into my head.

'Briars!'

I looked up to see Oswyn's weaselly face poking out of a window at the top of the gatehouse. Even from this distance I could see his arrogant expression. I wished I could scale the wall and punch him on the nose – but there was no ivy at all up to that window!

'Mister Scrope wants to know what you're up to, wandering about in the rain. As you're obviously not doing anything important for Master Cromwell, he says you'd better get back in. There's plenty of work to be done here.'

I knew this was no command from Mister Scrope. Hauling himself to his feet to look out of his window was too much for the Chief Scribe. He was more likely slumbering in his chair. I sauntered casually towards the gatehouse, irritated that Oswyn was commanding me to do the very thing I'd already intended to do. As I made for the scribes' room I wondered what Cromwell would say at my total lack of success in what should have been a simple task. I hoped he was too busy to come and ask me how I was getting on. I couldn't keep it from him for long though. He needed to know that the list of thefts was growing.

I gritted my teeth as I opened the office door. Oswyn

looked smug. 'Good to see you can do as you're told sometimes,' he said airily.

I stared pointedly at Mister Scrope who was snoring loudly. 'Clever man, our Chief Scribe,' I said solemnly. 'He can even give orders in his sleep!'

I sat down opposite Mark. 'You've missed some fun and games,' he whispered. 'Oswyn was trying to walk on his hands when Mister Scrope was out of the room.'

'Let me guess,' I whispered back. 'He wants to make the King laugh and win that money.'

'Well it made me laugh,' said Mark. 'Especially when he fell on his nose.'

'Did he hear you?' I asked, astonished at Mark's newfound bravery.

'Oh, no,' replied Mark, horrified. 'I pretended I was coughing.'

There was a knock on the door. Oswyn stood up importantly to open it. He returned with a note from a messenger. His eyes gleamed as he read it.

'Mister Scrope,' he bellowed. The Chief Scribe woke with a snort and looked wildly round. 'Master Cromwell wants to see Jack in the Presence Chamber.' Oswyn waved the paper in the Chief Scribe's face. 'It says 'urgent' in big letters. I wonder what that could be about, eh, Jack?' He was enjoying his moment of spite.

'Go quickly, Jack.' Mister Scrope waved me to the door and closed his eyes again.

I got up and took the message without a word. Mark looked as if this was the moment he'd always feared – me getting the sack, and Weasel-face's brother appearing in my place.

Oswyn was leaning back in his chair enjoying a pleasant daydream. 'I wonder if he's heard that one of his scribes was caught loitering in the rain instead of working – perhaps he's even told the King . . . Oh well, it will be one rival out of the way. Aycliffe's purse will be mine.'

Poor old Oswyn, I thought as I left the office. Little did he know that this particular scribe had very good reason for loitering in the rain. But my pleasure at this thought was short-lived. I knew exactly why Master Cromwell had summoned me. He wanted answers – and I had none to give him.

The Presence Chamber was even more crowded than usual and it took me a long time to find a route through. But it wasn't hard to find the King, raised above everyone on his platform. He was sitting in a gold chair with thick padded golden armrests, a tapestry woven in gold over his head and a gold carpet at his feet. His sumptuous robe was draped over his left shoulder and I could see that his arm rested in a silken sling.

Master Cromwell was at his side so I made for the platform. Clearly everyone had heard about the reward that Aycliffe and Shawe were offering and several brave souls were taking turns to try in vain to make King Henry laugh. By the scowl on the royal forehead, nothing was working.

Cromwell saw me and beckoned me to him. My master was always controlled in his manner, but today I could see that his patience was strained. The King suddenly barked at a couple of jesters who were doing some elaborate and not very funny capering. Cromwell winced as they sloped off, embarrassed. 'Well, Jack?' he asked, tight-lipped.

My answer wasn't going to please him. 'I am so sorry, sir,' I said. 'No one saw the thief go into the three chambers . . .'

'Three?' Cromwell looked astounded. 'What are you saying, Jack? There have been more thefts? Why was I not told?'

'They happened only a little while ago, sir,' I explained in a low voice. 'I went to investigate Lady Gooldsbury's theft as you asked, and while I was there, the other thefts were discovered in the next two rooms. Sir Basil and Lady Tresham have both been victims.'

'This is intolerable!' hissed my master, as the King let out a curse and sent a hapless servant scurrying away. 'I pray you have discovered who the miscreant is.'

I took a deep breath. 'No, sir. It's a mystery. It seems there is no way a thief could have got into those rooms.'

'Look again!'

'I will do everything in my power . . .'

'You certainly will!' snapped Cromwell. I was taken aback at his outburst. My master never showed his emotions. In fact I sometimes wondered if he had any, behind those heavy-lidded eyes.

He rubbed his forehead with his fingers. 'The King's injury has . . . worried me over the last few days.'

I knew perfectly well that it wasn't just His Majesty's ill temper that was worrying him.

'I'm sorry that I haven't found the culprit yet.'

'I believe you have done your best, Jack,' said Cromwell. 'Perhaps I've given you too great a task.'

A sharp pang of fear ran through me like a knife. If I failed to find a petty thief, I had no chance of being entrusted with whatever was really bothering my master.

'I will solve it, sir,' I told him.

'And I'm sure you believe that,' said Cromwell. 'I will give you until tomorrow.' He smiled wearily. 'However, if it proves to be beyond you then I must hand it on to someone more experienced.'

7

I could see from Cromwell's face that he meant every word. My gut twisted. I feared my master was losing faith in me. I had to show him I wasn't going to be beaten. I bowed and started to push my way to the door. He'd told me to look again. Well I would. However this time I had no valid reason to go into any of the rooms. I'd have to do it secretly. And for that I couldn't do without a lookout. Much as I hated to admit it, I needed Cat's help.

'Let Will Somers bring cheer, Sire.' A jolly voice rang out over the room as I tried to get to the door. 'A riddle to lighten your mood.'

I couldn't see the jester but my heart sank. Will Somers was a very clever man. If anyone could make the King laugh it would be him, and Aycliffe's purse would be won.

'Twelve pears hanging high, twelve men passing by,'

chanted Will Somers, as I battled through the crowd. 'Each took a pear and left eleven hanging there. How can this be?'

There was no immediate answer from the King.

I couldn't help thinking about the puzzle. Brother Matthew would challenge me with riddles from time to time. He said it was good to look at things sideways occasionally. Obviously face on, this riddle was impossible. If each man took a pear there would be none left. For the sum to work only one man could pick a pear. And then I had the answer. That was exactly what had happened. 'Each took a pear' was not all the men but just one man whose name was Each. I waited for the King to solve it too. Everyone knew he had a quick brain.

'Why do you torment me with these unsolvable puzzles?' came an angry bellow, then a yelp and the sound of something metal hitting the flagstones. I guessed that His Majesty had thrown his tankard at the jester.

The King must be in pain indeed if he couldn't work out a riddle before a lowly scribe. I was glad to be quitting the chamber and his bad temper. I sped off to find Cat. As I got near to her workroom I tried to think of a sewing emergency that would require the skills of my seamstress friend and no one else. I peeked round the open door.

All the workers had their heads bent over their work so no one saw me. Except Cat. She was hanging newly dyed skeins of thread on a line to dry. She spotted me hovering in the doorway. I beckoned to her and she gave a slight nod.

'God's oath!' she exclaimed, making everyone jump.

I ducked back into the corridor.

'I quite forgot,' I heard her say. 'Mistress Fairweather asked me to take a needle to her money pouch. It has a hole and she fears losing her coins.'

Cat was quick-witted, I'd give her that.

'Fetch it and bring it here.' That was Mr Wiltshire's voice. 'And hurry. You took long enough over your delivery this morning.'

I thought her master's order would have Cat stumped. I should have known better.

'Mistress Fairweather won't let me,' she said brightly. 'She's afraid to have anything out of her sight since the dreadful thefts. She said I must do it in her chamber or not at all.' Then I heard her gasp. 'But don't say I said anything about it. I was sworn to secrecy. She doesn't want anyone to know her fears for she says that a thief will target the weakest.'

This was good. Now Mr Wiltshire couldn't ask Mistress Fairweather about the mending and discover that Cat had made it up.

'Then go,' sighed her master. 'And don't dither about chatting this time.'

'Of course I won't,' said Cat.

She came out to join me in the corridor, her apron pockets bulging with sewing materials.

'I wouldn't have troubled you,' I said quickly. 'But I have to go back to the chambers where the thefts occurred and I need a lookout.'

'That's bilge water!' she laughed. 'You can't do without my expert snooping more like. I knew you'd be back.'

I didn't dignify that with a response. 'I'm going to have a look in Lord and Lady Tresham's bedchamber,' I told her. 'It'll be empty now they're off to find lodgings in Greenwich Village.'

'Empty apart from the Duke,' said Cat darkly. 'You definitely won't need a lookout if you're in that room. I bet my lady will have passed the word around and no one will go near it.' She sighed dramatically. 'But I said I'd help, so I won't let you down, even if it means being frightened to death.'

I knew that underneath it all, Cat couldn't bear to miss out!

Unfortunately the Treshams' chamber wasn't empty. They'd left their maidservant behind to pack their possessions. She sat on the floor, surrounded by chests and looking nervous.

'God be praised,' she gasped as she saw us. 'I thought you were Duke Humphrey come to get me. It's all very well for my mistress. She wants all her belongings stowed and gone from here in an hour and then she swans off and I'm the one who has to face the phantoms! I'm that scared I'm all butterfingers and so it's sure to take me longer than that.'

I was just wondering how to get her out of the room when Cat squatted down by her side.

'Don't be scared, Gwen,' she said. 'You're safe now we're here.'

I thought that was a bit rich after all the fuss she'd made on the way! But Cat hadn't finished.

'We'll help you,' she went on. 'Then you can leave all the quicker.'

Now I understood. It had been a clever move to get Gwen out of the way but I wasn't going to tell her that.

'Thank you,' said the maidservant. We all fell to folding and packing clothes into the chests. 'My mistress doesn't worry about me meeting Duke Humphrey. Oh no. Anyway, I don't know what *she's* so bothered about. If you ask me the ghost would take fright as soon as it saw her!'

Poor Gwen carried on in this vein right until the last stocking was packed.

'The carter will be here for these later,' she announced, kicking one of the chests.

Cat stared at the door after she'd gone. 'Sometimes I realise how lucky I am with my master. Mister Wiltshire's a good soul. Right, what are we going to do next?'

I pointed to the small, high window.

'I've been wondering if the thief could have come in from the roof,' I said. I stepped onto the chest that lay under the windowsill.

I leaned over the deep window ledge and twisted

round to look at the roof. Cat pushed up beside me.

'The eaves are a long way above,' I said. 'I can't see how anyone could get down to the room from there.'

'I've been in several palaces now,' said Cat thoughtfully as we scrambled back to the floor. 'But I don't remember any with walls this thick. These are unusual – you know, like a castle's walls – but Greenwich wasn't built as a castle. Windsor now, that's a proper castle. That's haunted too, so they say . . .'

I stopped listening. Something Cat had said got me wondering about the strange swishing noise she swore she'd heard earlier. There'd been nowhere for anyone to hide and make that sound except . . .

'You remember I've told you about old Brother Jerome,' I said.

'Back at the abbey.' Cat nodded. 'The one with lots of wise sayings.'

'And lots of stories,' I went on. 'He once said that when he was a young monk at some abbey in the North Country, prayers in the chapel were often disturbed by loud baaing and no one could understand why.'

'Ghost sheep?' whispered Cat, tremulously.

'No, it was real sheep,' I laughed. 'You see, once upon a time someone had built a hidden passage in the wall but the chapel was so old that it had been forgotten.'

Cat fixed me with a stare. 'What's that got to do with sheep?'

'The other end was in an outer wall and the bricks had all crumbled away. The sheep found it, trotted along and decided to join in with the prayers.'

'You're making that up!' she declared.

'No, it's true,' I said. 'And anyway, the sheep aren't the important thing. What I'm trying to tell you is that there could be a hidden passage here. The walls are thick enough. And it would mean that it wasn't a ghost who did the thefts. It was a living, breathing robber who popped in and out of the walls.'

We inspected the wall below the window. Like the others in the chamber, it was covered in carved wooden panelling, decorated above with a row of vines.

I knocked on the wood. 'Does that sound hollow to you?' I asked Cat.

'It does,' she breathed.

I could see the excited look in her eyes.

'There must be some way of getting into it,' I said. 'Some sort of door.'

Frantically we ran our hands over the wooden stems, leaves and grapes. I prodded and probed but everything was solid under my fingers. I ran my hands up every join in the panelling but it was all firmly fixed.

'Come here, Jack,' said Cat. She was kneeling by the bed. 'This bunch of grapes feels different from the others. It's a bit loose.'

Cat was right. When I grasped it, it moved under my fingers. I gave it a twist. Nothing happened. I pushed it. Still nothing.

'Maybe it's just a fault in the carving,' suggested Cat.

I nodded. I'd let Brother Jerome's story run away with me. In desperation I gave it a tug.

There was a noise like someone clicking their fingers.

The grapes sprung back into position.

A dark line appeared in the panel below, stretching from the floor to the top of the wood.

'It's an opening,' whispered Cat. 'We've found a hidden passage!'

8

I slid the panel open and peered into the mysterious, musty-smelling dark. I took a candle from beside the bed, lit it and shone it into the hole. To the right the passage ended in a stone wall. To the left, the passage stretched away into the distance.

'Let me see!' Cat nearly bowled me over in her eagerness to get a look. I moved over and she stuck her head in. 'So this is how the thief got into the room. Where does it lead?'

'That's what we're about to find out. We'd better keep our voices down, for I wager it goes to Sir Basil's and Lady Gooldsbury's rooms.'

Cat followed me through the opening, sliding the panel closed behind her.

The outer wall of the passage was made of rough brick. The other wall and the roof were made of wood. The passage was tall enough for a man to stand without stooping, but as we moved along we soon came to a place where the ceiling was so low we had to get down on our hands and knees.

'There must be a window above us!' I whispered. 'So that's why they're so high on this stretch of wall.'

'Obviously,' replied Cat. 'If they were the usual height, no one would be able to pass along here at all!'

I made for a tiny circle of light that shone through a small hole in the wooden wall. As I put my eye to the hole I discovered it had a round piece of glass inserted in it, like a very small spectacle lens. Through it I could see a neat row of riding boots and a bed with perfectly straight velvet hangings.

'I was right,' I whispered. 'It's Sir Basil's room.'

'Are you sure?' asked Cat.

'Of course I'm sure,' I said. Below the hole I could feel the top of a panel which I guessed would slide away like the first one we'd found.

'Let's carry on,' I whispered.

Ducking under the next window, I came to another sliding panel. I peered through the tiny spyhole above it. This chamber was stuffed full of furniture, every piece covered in lacy cloths, fussy little angel statues and china kittens.

'Lady Gooldsbury's?' whispered Cat.

I nodded.

In the dim light it looked as though the passageway ended a little further along. So, I reasoned, it went between the three rooms where the thefts had occurred.

I wondered if one of the servants had discovered the hidden path in the wall. It was more likely to be a lowborn thief than a courtier. As Cat had said, the stolen items were only riches to someone poor.

But when I held the candle up its light showed that the darkness at the end had hidden a corner. I beckoned to Cat, who was standing on tiptoes and nosily peering into her ladyship's chamber. We crept round the corner into a short stretch of passage, blocked by a wall.

'Help me look for a door,' I whispered in Cat's ear. 'There has to be one at this end otherwise the passage would have stopped at Lady Gooldsbury's room.'

I shone the candle over the wall. Cat felt the panelling. She straightened and poked me in the ribs. I managed not to yelp – she had sharp fingers.

'I've found one,' she hissed. 'Shall I open it?'

'No!' I whispered. 'We don't know who might be on the other side! There must be a spy hole here too.'

We found the pinprick of light above the panel. I peered through and almost gasped in surprise. In front of my eye was the most sumptuous bedchamber I'd ever seen. Gold columns, rich velvet hangings and jewelled statues filled my view.

'What can you see?' pestered Cat.

I stepped aside and she gave a low whistle as she took in the amazing sight. 'Someone's showing off their riches!' she murmured. 'This is very strange. No one else has reported a theft but if I was a thief this would have been the first room I'd have had a poke about in!'

'Unless this is the thief's own room,' I said.

'It can't be,' said Cat. 'Why steal trifles when you have so much already? It doesn't make sense.'

'It does if the thief is a servant who works in here,' I said. 'We need to look around. Is the room empty?'

'Think so,' Cat replied. She put her ear to the wood. 'Sounds empty too.'

I placed the candle on the floor of the passage. We slid the panel across, crept through and closed it. We started in fear at the sight of two figures creeping towards us.

Cat laughed. 'We're scared of our own reflections! Look around – we're everywhere!'

Between the tapestries and portraits, mirrors covered the walls, making the chamber appear even larger than it was. Each time we moved all our images moved too.

A huge bed stood in the centre of the room, hung with gold drapes and covered with a silk counterpane.

Cat lifted the counterpane. 'Eight mattresses!' she gasped. 'You'd need a ladder to climb into that!'

She ran over to gawp at a clock standing on a marble pillar. Three golden dials were surrounded by the numbers picked out in gilt. The face was decorated with tiny red flowers and I'd have bet the palace that every single one was a priceless ruby.

'We should search,' I said. 'It would be easy for a

servant to hide the things here. His master or mistress would never notice.'

I began rifling through a box of fine gloves, keeping my eye on the door.

We hunted through the riches in the chamber, placing each thing back exactly as we'd found it, ears pricked for anyone approaching. There were plenty of places a servant could hide his ill-gotten gains. In one of the chests, or a jewel-encrusted box on a table, or even stuffed behind a tapestry.

Then something caught my eye, something half hidden under the huge bed. 'What's that?'

'It's just a chamber pot,' said Cat. 'Surely the thief wouldn't hide anything in there.'

'Not the chamber pot! There's something behind it.' I dived down, slid past the porcelain pot and retrieved a silver casket. It wasn't locked. I lifted the lid.

We both stared for a moment at the missing ring, fan and French hood.

'We just need to find out whose bedchamber this is,' I said. 'Then we'll know which servants to suspect.'

'There could be initials on some of the jewellery,' said Cat, picking up a chain heavy with diamonds. 'This must be worth a king's ransom.'

She suddenly dropped it as if it was on fire. 'No! . . . It can't be . . .'

'What have you found?' I asked.

Cat had gone whiter than the sheets on the bed. She looked round wildly. 'It's just dawned on me

whose room this is,' she whispered. 'We need to go . . .
now!'

'Why?' I asked. 'What do you mean?'

'I've been in many courtiers' rooms,' she said, 'and
though some are grand, none are as splendid as this
one.'

My stomach lurched as I finally understood. 'Are
you telling me . . . ?'

She nodded. 'I reckon we're in the King's bedchamber.
We need to go now. We can't risk being caught.'

Before we could move, we heard a shout. Then heavy
footsteps. Now the rattle of a latch. Without a word,
Cat and I scrambled up the eight mattresses onto the
bed and hid behind its curtains as the door was flung
open.

'Insolent dolts!' came a deep, booming voice. 'I tell
you, I wish to be left in peace in my own chamber!'

I felt Cat tremble beside me.

We were in big trouble.

9

Terror made the blood thump so loudly in my ears that I couldn't hear anything else. With a shaking hand, I edged the curtain aside a little so we could both peep through. There seemed to be a whole army of King Henrys in the room. He paced angrily up and down in front of the mirrors, his reflections looking even larger and more menacing than he was. I didn't envy Master Cromwell telling the King that one of his servants was a thief. His Majesty's temper did not need fuelling.

As we watched he punched the wall, thumped a couple of cushions, then suddenly stopped and dropped to his knees. For a second I thought he was going to pray, but soon realised he was grovelling under the bed. I was astonished to see him pull out the casket!

A secretive grin crept over his face. Secretive grins crept over the faces of the mirror army as a multitude of kings fingered the seal ring, the fan and the French hood.

I heard a tiny intake of breath and Cat squeezed my arm so hard I nearly cried out. King Henry himself was the thief! I could not for the life of me imagine why our monarch, surely the richest man in England, would go thieving.

Now the King was putting everything back in the box and pushing it under the bed. I hoped that the sight of his plunder would put him in a good mood and he'd go off in search of company. I was wrong. He paced the room again, rubbing his injured shoulder.

'Will this infernal wound never heal?' he bellowed in sudden temper, kicking a footstool and sending it spinning across the floor. Then he picked up a book and slung it angrily at the bed. It hit our curtain, pushing it aside. He only had to look our way and he'd see a gibbering seamstress and scribe.

Luckily there was a faint tap on the door.

'Who disturbs me now?' growled His Majesty.

I eased the curtain over us again.

'If it please your Grace,' came a timid servant's voice, 'Miles Hawkesworth craves a word with you.'

'What does he want?' grunted the King.

'He says he has almost finished copying out your new piece of music. He begs that your Grace spare him some time to discuss the last section.'

'Ah, now that is most welcome!' exclaimed the King, suddenly sounding pleased. I was astonished by how his mood could change in an instant. 'I am about to dine in the Presence Chamber. Master Cromwell has informed me that he has organised some entertainment for later this evening. Tell Mister Hawkesworth that he will have my attention between food and tumblers!'

Cat and I waited a while after the door had closed. His Majesty could easily change his mind and come storming back in. When we were sure it was safe we scuttled out and were soon hurrying along the hidden passage and tumbling into Lady Tresham's room. I snuffed out the candle and we looked at each other in the faint afternoon light.

'I thought I was dreaming!' gasped Cat. 'I was so scared and it was so funny and the room was so amazing and I didn't know whether to laugh or cry but I couldn't do either and . . .'

'You should be thankful we weren't caught,' I interrupted. If I let her, I knew Cat would go over the scene a hundred times. I wondered if other girls had as much to say on every subject as Cat Thimblebee. I had no idea. She was the only girl I knew.

'So that was the King we heard in the wall, not a ghost,' said Cat. 'I reckon he's doing it because he's bored. He's usually really busy with his archery and his tennis and his riding—'

'When a certain seamstress isn't borrowing his horse!' I put in.

'You know I only take Diablo now His Majesty won't ride him,' said Cat. 'Poor Diablo, just because he was a present from Queen Katherine and the King wants to be married to Lady Anne Boleyn instead. That's not Diablo's fault. Anyway, it seems to me that King Henry is so fed up with his injury that he's out to cause mischief. He's so like my youngest brother Benjamin. I used to sit on Ben in church to stop him climbing up the pillars during the sermons.'

'I think you have the King's motive, Cat,' I said. 'I must tell my master without delay. Though I wonder if he'll believe me.'

'You won't tell him we spied on the royal bedchamber, will you?' gasped Cat. 'That would be treason, surely.'

'I don't think . . .' I began.

'And you definitely can't tell him we hid behind his bed curtains. That could be treason too.'

'I'm not sure that sitting on the royal bed could be called trea—'

'In fact,' said Cat in sudden horror, 'you can't tell Master Cromwell anything. If calling the King a thief isn't treason, I don't know what is!'

I had no answer. If I told Master Cromwell what we'd discovered, I realised I'd be in some sort of trouble for criticising the monarch. No one spoke a word against the King. Not if they valued their freedom. Yet Cromwell had charged me with this task. I could not go against my orders.

Or could I? The secret work of Cromwell's band of spies was to protect His Majesty and keep him safe. Well, I reasoned, the King was in no danger from a thief. He *was* the thief! That surely let me off the hook. My moment of relief was short-lived.

'If I can't tell Cromwell, he'll think I've failed,' I said miserably.

'Then you'll have to go straight to the King,' laughed Cat. She made a mock bow. 'Excuse me, Sire,' she said, facing the floor, 'I know it was you who pinched all that stuff!'

I began to smile at her little show and then stopped short. 'That's exactly what I'm going to do.'

'What?' exclaimed Cat, whipping her head up.

'I'm going to tell the King that I know he's the thief,' I declared.

Cat laughed. 'And I'll come and visit you in the Tower!'

'I won't exactly accuse him,' I insisted. 'I'm going to tell him how clever he's been. Then hopefully he'll let me tell my master.'

'Good luck with that,' said Cat.

'I don't need your luck,' I said airily. 'You can help me with something though.'

'Can I?' Cat sounded suspicious.

'Tell me who Miles Hawkesworth is. I've not come across him before.'

'That's because you're tone deaf and don't you deny it. I've heard you sing. Mister Hawkesworth is the Court Composer and for all he makes nice tunes, he's a funny, fussy little thing. If his shirts aren't folded just so after mending, he sends them back! Many's the time I've been tempted to do it wrong simply to annoy him.'

'I did see a puny man at luncheon today, humming to himself and scribbling down music,' I said.

'That'll be him,' snorted Cat. 'In a world of his own. Well, I can't stand here gossiping all evening. I'll see you tomorrow up the hill for your riding lesson.'

She was gone in an instant. I slipped out behind her. The King had said he'd be in the Presence Chamber so now was the time to try to get to him.

'Make way!' came a cry. Men clad in bright chequered costumes came running past me. The acrobats had arrived – and they weren't going to be stopped by the guards. I joined the group, waving my arms and skipping like them. I thought I'd passed unnoticed until a lance blocked my way. I looked up into the face of Nicholas Mountford.

'What are you up to, Jack?' The giant yeoman was grinning down at me. 'Have you stopped scribing and joined the tumblers? It wouldn't surprise me. You led me a merry dance climbing the walls of Whitehall.'

Whenever I saw Nicholas Mountford, he always reminded me about our first meeting. Because of a small misunderstanding, he'd chased me all over the palace – until I climbed out of a window and jumped off some handy scaffolding!

'The acrobats could at least have found you a proper costume!' he added.

'And taught him not to look like a demented puppet,' laughed his companion.

'You're not thinking of going in, are you, Jack?' asked Mister Mountford. 'All the world and his wife are there. If the King of Spain himself came along I wouldn't be able to let him through.'

I thought quickly. I couldn't say I wanted a word with His Majesty. They'd believe I truly was demented. 'I only wanted to watch the entertainment,' I told them. 'I've never seen anything like it before.' That was true. The nearest I'd got to tumbling at the abbey was when Father Busbrig pushed me down the chapel steps. I put on my saddest face and peeked round the guards. The acrobats were cartwheeling about the room, their feet narrowly missing the noses of the courtiers. The King was the only person in the room not laughing. The purse was still there to be won although that would have to wait. I had a more important – and possibly disastrous – mission to carry out. I gave the guards an appealing look.

'Go on then,' said Mountford. 'You're skinny enough. But don't tell anyone I let you in.'

'And keep to the back,' added his friend.

I thanked them. Now to get to the King. No sign of Cromwell. That was good. While the acrobats formed a human pyramid, I slipped along behind the solid wall of rapt courtiers. No one was taking any notice of me as I pushed my way towards the back of the royal chair. The flattering compliments I'd prepared in my mind paled before the glorious sight of His Majesty in his golden splendour.

I'd just thought of suggesting that all the riches in the world were nothing compared with the King's glittering wit, when a plump, be-ringed hand grasped my arm.

I cursed inwardly. It was Master Cromwell – the very person I didn't want to meet.

'I assume you're here to see me, Jack,' he said sternly. 'I hope you have news.'

'Er . . . I came to tell you that I'm making progress, sir,' I burbled.

'I am pleased to hear it.' I realised he was waiting for the details.

'I would not wish to take you from the entertainment, sir.'

'You wouldn't. My mind was not on it.'

At once I was reminded of the grave look that Aycliffe had given me when he'd hinted at a deeper, more serious matter than my investigation. Again I had a helpless yearning to be part of whatever it was. Something that threatened the safety of the country? I knew that Spain was angry with King Henry because he wanted to divorce his Spanish queen, Katherine. Was it something to do with that? All around us were cries of amazement as the tumblers tossed each other into the air. But Cromwell kept his unblinking eyes fixed on my face. 'Time is running out. We cannot keep this from His Majesty for ever. Do I need to brief someone else?'

'You must trust me, sir,' I pleaded. 'There are reasons why I cannot tell you more now. I'll have an answer for you soon!'

'I require that answer by tomorrow noon.' My master gazed at me steadily. I hated that look. It made me feel as if he was reading my thoughts.

I had no choice but to leave. I bowed and made for the door. There was no way I was going to get a private word with the King tonight. I'd have my work cut out tomorrow. I had to accuse my esteemed sovereign of being a thief without actually accusing him, and all before the clock struck twelve.

10

I slept very badly. All night I dreamed that I poured compliment after compliment into His Majesty's ear. And it was all going very well until the moment when I dared to call him a thief. In an instant I was being marched towards the executioner's block while Master Cromwell told everyone that he'd always known I was a bad lot. It was a relief to wake!

The sun was just rising as I climbed the hill behind the palace for my riding lesson. With every step I fretted about what I was going to say to the King. After my nightmare I had no faith in my powers of flattery! Indeed old Brother Jerome always said that dreams bore a message and you ignored them at your peril. There had to be a way to tell His Majesty that I knew what he'd been up to, without getting my head cut off. I had another problem. How was I going to convince Mister Scrope to let me leave the office yet again? I convinced myself I would come up with something . . . at least, I hoped I would!

There was a tower at the top of the hill – a big square keep with lots of windows and a turret on top. It must have been a very good place for an army to keep a lookout. I could see the palace far below and London Town and the hills beyond. Near the tower stood a round stone building, not much taller than me. I had no idea what that was – probably the soldiers' privies. I paced round the tower, waiting for Cat, worrying that the King might stay in his rooms all morning and I'd have no chance for an audience with him.

'Jack!' Cat was beckoning to me from a nearby copse of trees. A huge black stallion stood next to her. It was Diablo, the devil horse. Well, he was a devil when I got on his back. *If only the King hadn't taken against his Spanish wife*, I thought to myself, *I wouldn't have to ride Diablo!*

'Come away from there!' called Cat.

'Why?' I asked, going over to join her. 'There's no one here to see me.'

'No one human,' said Cat darkly. 'You wouldn't get me inside for a basketful of gold. It's haunted!'

'Which ghost is this?' I asked.

'Duke Humphrey, you pudding brain,' Cat told me. 'It's his tower. Some say he met a violent end up there, not long after he'd had it built. His legs were chopped off and he was thrown from the top.'

'That's not what you said yesterday!' I exclaimed.

'You said he was murdered in Greenwich Palace and that his ghost walks there.'

'I reckon he haunts everywhere,' she whispered, giving the tower an anxious glance. 'I don't want him popping up and rattling his blood-stained chains at me – or waving his severed legs from the window.'

'You never said he had chains.'

'Stands to reason,' said Cat. 'All ghosts have chains.'

She helped me up onto Diablo's fancy saddle. I took the reins and squeezed the stallion's flanks with my legs while my instructor watched. The horse refused to move. Although I couldn't see Cat's face I knew she was bursting to keep from laughing.

'Still a lot of work to do,' she chirped. 'I'll lead you round the beacon.' We set off for the stone building.

'So that's a beacon,' I said as Diablo took me past. Twigs and branches were sticking out of the open roof. 'Aren't beacons lit to warn of an invasion? I'd love to see one alight.'

'Well I wouldn't,' scoffed Cat. 'It would mean we're being attacked. You're like my brothers – they love mucking about with bonfires.'

She took Diablo's halter and made him trot and walk by turns. I wobbled about in the saddle. 'You're not putting your mind to the task,' she scolded. 'You have to concentrate every second if you want to improve.'

'It's not that I can't do it,' I told her. 'It's just that my head is full of other things.'

'Let me guess,' said Cat. 'You haven't thought of a

way to tell the King that you've discovered his little game.'

'Yes I have,' I lied.

'I was thinking you could do a riddle!' suggested Cat. 'I've heard His Majesty loves a good riddle.'

'You wouldn't have thought so if you'd seen him when Will Somers tried one!' I replied, determined not to let Cat know she'd thought of a good idea.

Because I'd realised that a riddle might just work. I'd make sure I invented one that the King, and only the King, understood – and I'd make sure he got it straight away, before he had the chance to chuck a tankard at me.

Cat let go of the bridle. 'Now, to finish, you go round on your own,' she instructed.

My mind was already working on a possible subject for my puzzle, but I squeezed my legs and to my surprise, Diablo obeyed! We set off at a trot which jolted every bone in my body. But at least I was staying on. I steered my steed round the tower. Well, Diablo decided that was the way to go and I had to go with him. Then Diablo decided to go faster.

'Cat!' I cried. 'I've forgotten how to make him stop!'

In the end I didn't need to. Diablo did it for me. The trouble was, he didn't give me any warning. He skidded to a halt next to a nice juicy patch of grass. I flew out of the saddle, somersaulted through the air and landed on my bum on the hard ground. Diablo carried on munching.

'Hmmm!' said Cat, chuckling as she ran up and vaulted expertly onto Diablo's back. 'Looks like you've forgotten how to dismount too.'

And with that she galloped off down the hill.

I sat there, watching her go, my pride as sore as my bottom. It didn't help that a pair of noisy magpies was sitting in a tree overhead. It sounded as if they were having a good laugh at my expense. I went to shake my fist at them and then an idea flew into my head. Magpies stole shiny things and took them to their nests. Just like the King!

Now I knew exactly what my riddle would be about.

'Thank you, Mr and Mrs Magpie,' I said.

11

After breakfast I set to my work. At least I made out I was working, head bent over the endless chandlery accounts. It seemed that the Court went through a mountain of candles! When no one was looking I scribbled ideas for my riddle onto a discarded scrap of parchment. As fast as I wrote a line, I scored it through. Somehow I had to get the magpies into the puzzle. And it had to be really clever if I was going to avoid the wrath of the King.

'Jack!' whispered Mark urgently. 'Oswyn's watching you. Stop sucking your quill and try and look as if you're working or he'll get you into trouble with Mister Scrope.'

This was daring for Mark. He would not usually be content until I was *actually* doing what I was supposed to. He was obviously learning some of my tricky ways.

'Thanks, Mark,' I whispered back, giving Weasel-face a quick glance. He was glaring at me. 'To tell you the truth, I'm making up a riddle.'

Mark looked puzzled.

'For the King.'

Mark looked horrified. 'Why?'

I had my explanation ready. 'I want to make him laugh and win that purse.' I couldn't tell Mark the real reason.

'Well, good luck,' my friend muttered, shaking his head in disbelief. 'You'll need it if you're going anywhere near His Majesty. Tell me how you get on . . . if you survive.'

'I'll do my best.'

'It will be better than Oswyn's attempt,' Mark went on.

'What's he tried now? Standing on his head? Eating fire?'

'He's been practising his singing,' said Mark with a shudder of horror.

I laughed, but inside I was trying to shake the wool that seemed to be clogging up my head. If only I could find a way to bring in the King and the magpies so that only His Majesty would recognise my double meaning.

And with that the words came to me. I shot out of my chair.

'Whatever's the matter?' called Mister Scrope.

'He has ants in his breeches,' said Oswyn nastily. 'He hasn't done any work all morning.'

'I heard someone at the door,' I said, inventing wildly. I hurried over before anyone could doubt my words, opened it a crack and had a conversation with an imaginary messenger. 'Master Cromwell needs some papers,' I told Mister Scrope, 'and requests that I bring them to him.'

Oswyn's eyes narrowed. 'I didn't hear a knock,' he said. 'Besides I'm the one who should be doing Master Cromwell's bidding. I've been here the longest. By rights, I should be senior scribe.'

I didn't give him a chance to get up, but snatched a random bundle of letters and made for the door. I was sorry to give Weasel-face more reason for hating me and wishing me gone, but it couldn't be helped.

Mister Scrope called me back. I turned, thinking my ruse to get to the King hadn't worked after all. He was waving some documents at me. 'As you're going, take these too. They require His Majesty's signature.'

Relieved, I picked up a penner, making sure that there was ink in its pot and the quills inside the long leather tube were well trimmed. I hooked the strings over my belt and hurried down to the Presence Chamber, perfecting the words of my riddle. As I edged through the crowd to where Master Cromwell stood beside the King's chair, my confidence waned a little. His Majesty was clearly not one whit cheered by the little bunch of singers trilling 'Hey nonny nonny' at him. We all winced when he bellowed at them to leave him alone.

Robert Aycliffe and Francis Shawe stood nearby. They seemed to be in the middle of some light-hearted conversation, Aycliffe showing none of the secret worry that I suspected was pressing on him.

The King's robe and doublet were arranged so that his bandaged shoulder was clearly visible. There was fresh blood on the bandage and that worried me. I'd seen plenty of injuries at the abbey, for all the local people came to Brother Francis, the apothecary, with their ailments. He would ensure that any break in the skin was helped to heal as quickly as possible to prevent it putrefying. Yet the King's didn't seem to be healing. I wondered if he was heeding the advice of his physicians and resting his shoulder. I doubted it.

After the Hey nonnies, no one else was daring to venture near the King. It's now or never, I told myself, my stomach lurching in fright.

'Jack!'

I'd been waylaid again. Master Cromwell was beckoning to me.

'From your expression, I gather you still have no news,' he said sourly, taking the papers I gave him and putting them on a nearby table. Although he looked calm, his hands were clenched tightly together. 'I hope you weren't lying when you said you'd know by noon . . .'

'Forgive me, sir,' I said before he could finish. 'I do have something to tell you.' I took a deep breath. 'But first I beg leave to speak to His Majesty.'

'You must have a death wish, Jack,' replied Cromwell. 'You can see how things stand with the King.'

'I assure you that this will help,' I said, hoping desperately that it would.

Cromwell shrugged. 'Then I have to trust you.'

I stepped towards the King, trying not to tremble, and bowed deeply.

'What do you want?' he growled. It was all I could do not to run. Then he peered at me more closely and seized my arm painfully hard. 'I recognise you, Jack Briars,' he hissed in my ear. 'You may have done me some small service in the past but that does not give you permission to pester me whenever you wish.'

I wasn't sure whether the 'small service' was when I amused him with the pies or the time when I saved his life. I couldn't ask, of course.

'I have no wish to pester you, my Liege,' I said with another bow. 'I have a riddle to lift your spirits.'

The King glared at me, Cromwell started forwards as if to stop me and several people nearby backed away so as not to be hurt in the explosion to come!

I launched into it before I lost my nerve. 'Three little treasures are lost. The first adorned a head. The second did grace a hand. The third did cool a cheek. And all to be found within a royal magpie's nest.'

I waited for his response. The King's face went white then red and his eyes narrowed. I knew he had got the meaning of my puzzle and now I wished he hadn't.

12

I fell to my knees, head bowed, waiting to hear my fate. The King wheezed. Had I caused him to have an apoplexy?

He wheezed again, even louder this time. The guards were going to throw me in the palace dungeon. But when I dared to look up I saw there was a smile playing round His Majesty's lips. He pulled me to my feet, the smile spreading over his face.

Then he threw back his head and roared – with laughter. His whole body shook and tears ran down his face. I suddenly realised that I was safe from the dungeon, and even better, I was going to win Aycliffe and Shawe's prize!

'By George,' he managed at last. 'That is a fine riddle, Jack Briars, and one to which I have the answer.'

God's oath! Was he going to admit his guilt to the whole Court?

But the King waved his hand at the nearby courtiers. 'Give us some room. I would have a private word with this young scribe. He has given me an idea. We are going to devise a riddle for my sweet Lady Anne.'

I couldn't believe that I, abbey boy and foundling, was now being invited to have a private word with King Henry.

'The riddle making is merely a pretence,' he murmured when everyone else had withdrawn. 'I have a song almost ready for my lady. Tell me, how did you know I was the thief? I can't believe you would get past my guards to enter my Privy Bedchamber.' He pinched my arm. 'And you're flesh and blood, not a phantom able to pass through walls.'

'Master Cromwell asked me to investigate the thefts,' I said. 'He wanted to keep you from irritation so it had to be done quietly. I have not told him who the culprit is.'

The King looked over at Cromwell. 'I am grateful that Thomas is so diligent on my behalf,' he said. 'And grateful to you for keeping my secret. Go on.'

'While I was searching for clues, I stumbled upon a hidden passage. I reasoned that as it went between certain chambers, a royal magpie could flit in and out without being discovered.'

He didn't look surprised. I wondered if he'd been waiting for me to admit this.

'You are to mention secret passages to no one, do

75

you understand?' he whispered. 'Not even Master Cromwell.'

'Yes, Sire.' I thought of Cat and was relieved he didn't ask me if anyone else knew of my discovery.

'I found the passage when I was a young boy,' the King went on conspiratorially. 'I was playing hide and seek with my sisters. I always won after that, of course, as no one thought to look for me in the walls themselves.' He sighed. 'It's only a short passage but you can imagine the tricks I played, disappearing from one bedroom and reappearing in one of the other three.'

'It must have been such fun, Sire,' I said. I began to imagine doing that at my old home in the abbey. I could have popped up and frightened Father Busbrig into a fit!

'I forgot all about it until yesterday,' the King continued. 'As I sat in my chamber, bored beyond belief and wearied to death by the fussing physicians, I remembered the hidden passage. When they bustled out to fetch some new cursed remedy or other I slipped through the door in the panelling. I merely intended to surprise them when they returned to find an empty chair instead of their monarch! But once in the passage I had another idea. I decided to play the thief. You cannot imagine what delight it is to act out a deception, Jack.'

I bowed. I could not tell him how well I understood. But where he spoke of acting a part for jest, I'd had to make mine real. Not so long ago I'd faced cold-hearted murderers in order to save his life. One moment the excitement was exhilarating, the next it turned to icy terror.

'My expedition to the first two chambers was quick and simple,' explained the King. 'I returned to my bedchamber and slipped back in before my doctors had returned. I waited in secret glee, hoping that someone would bring me news of the thefts. For what is the point of a jest if you do not see its effect? As I heard nothing I went off on another forage. This time I made for Sir Rowland and Lady Tresham's chamber. I was certain that her ladyship would waste no time in letting the whole palace know what had happened.'

'Instead, Sire, she decided a phantom had stolen her fan,' I told him, 'and whisked her husband off to stay elsewhere.'

'Curse the woman for not making more of a fuss!' The King touched his bandaged shoulder. 'So my efforts were all in vain. And I managed to reopen my wound on the way back. It's a tight squeeze for a man of my strong build.'

So that's why Cat had heard the swishing and the moan, I thought. *No ghost but a king playing tricks. And it explains why there is fresh blood on the bandage.*

'I will be making sure that the door at my end cannot be opened from now on,' said King Henry and I detected a warning note in his voice. 'I don't want any more scribes visiting unannounced.' He looked about.

'Where is Cromwell?' My master came forward. 'I commend your . . . scribe to you.'

Cromwell was usually very good at keeping his feelings to himself but I could see his puzzlement.

Then something happened that I still cannot believe – indeed I wonder if it was just a trick of the candlelight. The King winked at me.

'It seems, good Thomas,' he continued in a low voice, 'that there have been some petty thefts here at Court.'

'Thefts, Sire?' he asked as if this was news to him. His tone was all innocent puzzlement.

'To speak truly, theft is too strong a word,' the King told him. 'Your scribe found a magpie's nest – a magpie with a damaged wing – and inside were all the missing items.'

Cromwell looked from me to the King and back again. There was a pause, then he gave me the slightest of nods. With relief, I realised he'd understood the King's words.

'That is good news,' he said simply. 'Well done, Jack.'

His gaze was steady but it warmed me like a fire on a cold winter's day.

Cromwell bowed his head to the King. 'Will the . . . bird be punished, Sire?' he asked, joining in with the coded conversation. I imagine that inside he would like to have strangled His Majesty for the trouble he'd caused!

'He has had punishment enough, I think,' replied the King, rubbing his shoulder. 'Now leave me.'

As we bowed and moved away I knew I owed Master Cromwell some sort of explanation about the thefts, though I wasn't sure how I could tell him anything without mentioning the hidden passage. I was about to speak to him when Aycliffe approached.

'Well done, young sir!' he said, holding up a purse. 'You won this fair and square, though I can't for the life of me see what was so funny about that riddle. Indeed, I don't quite understand it.'

I didn't know how to answer this but luckily I was saved by Francis Shawe. 'Are you paying your debt, Robert?' he asked, coming to join us. 'Then let me put in my share.'

He added five more coins to the purse and handed it to me. Ten silver sixpences. I'd never had so much money in my life. In fact, I'd never had any money!

'Thank you,' I gasped, tying it to my belt. My thoughts were racing. I could buy a sword, or a dagger or dozens of those huge sugared buns from the bakers in Greenwich Village . . .

Two heralds blasted their trumpets for silence. King Henry got to his feet.

'I understand that there have been some petty thefts at Court,' he announced.

Everyone looked at his neighbour in alarm. Who could have told the King?

'And I want to put your minds at rest,' he went on. 'The culprit was simply a magpie and the missing items are in his nest. I will command someone to climb up and retrieve the valuables. And I will command the bird to steal no more!'

There was a cheer, although I caught a few puzzled glances. King Henry sat, enjoying the attention.

'This would be a good time to have those papers signed,' said Cromwell's voice in my ear. 'He's in a better humour, thanks to you. Fetch them and we'll strike while the iron is hot.'

As I stood beside my master, holding the inkpot and quill ready, the thin man I'd seen scribbling at lunch, appeared at his side. I thought Cromwell would only deal with the Court Composer after the important business with the King was finished, but he turned immediately.

'What is it, Miles?'

'I fear someone has been in my room this morning,' replied Mister Hawkesworth, fingering his sleeves anxiously. I could just pick out his words, for he spoke in a low voice as if he only wanted Cromwell to hear.

He reminded me of Mark and his imagined worries and I waited for my master to laugh this off. But to my surprise he looked concerned. Something more important was going on here. I listened hard.

'Was anything taken?' he asked quietly.

Miles shook his head. 'Nothing is gone,' he said, 'but I thought you would want to know.'

Cromwell said nothing in reply but took me aside.

'You seem to know more about the royal magpie than I do, Jack. Is it possible that the . . . bird visited rooms on the ground floor too? The Court Composer's chamber for instance?'

'Absolutely not, sir,' I said. Cromwell looked surprised at my certainty, but I couldn't tell him I'd found that the hidden passage only linked the three bedrooms with the King's. Then I had a happy thought. 'The magpie's wing is troubling him too much to take him so far.'

'I see.' Cromwell turned again to Mister Hawkesworth and they exchanged more muttered words, but I couldn't catch them. My master looked grave. Was this something to do with the business that had been worrying him and Aycliffe so much? Was Mister Hawkesworth involved in some way? Each of Cromwell's spies knew little about the others, but I felt some surprise that this nervous man could have anything to do with the secret workings of the network. Yet if Hawkesworth wasn't involved, then why was Cromwell so obviously concerned that someone had been in his chamber? There was no chance to hear more, for a shout interrupted their talk.

'Miles!' It was the King. 'How is my song coming along? Have you made the changes we discussed?'

Miles scuttled away to His Majesty and they began an earnest conversation.

It came to me that my investigation was over. Cromwell was not going to let me in on the other –

and more important – problem that was worrying him. There was nothing more to do than go back to work, and to the anger of Weasel-face who'd hate me even more when he found out I'd won the purse.

A servant hurried up to the Court Composer as he finished speaking to the King.

'There's been a delivery for you, Mister Hawkesworth,' said the servant. 'I've left it in your room and come to tell you just as you ordered.' Miles nodded. 'A new score has arrived from my old music teacher,' he told Cromwell. 'I will ask His Majesty's leave to go and study it directly.'

'Please do,' replied Cromwell. 'I would be most interested to hear it when it is ready for performance.'

I saw the composer bow nervously before the King as he made his request.

'Permission, Mister Hawkesworth?' shouted the King, red with sudden anger. The room went silent. 'What of the royal music, sirrah? Are you to be distracted by any old fool who sends you trifling compositions?'

'I beg your pardon, Sire,' gabbled the Court Composer, backing away from his monarch's wrath. 'I did not mean . . .'

He tailed off and I noted that he looked to Master Cromwell as if for help. But Cromwell made no move.

The King rose to his feet, swiping the papers and ink from the table.

'Go and trifle with your stupid music!' His eyes blazed round the room. 'And as for the rest of you simpering fools, clear this chamber, and leave me alone!'

13

There was a second of complete silence and then the courtiers were all bowing and backing away from the King. If I hadn't been worried about angering His Majesty, I'd have laughed out loud at the sight of them getting stuck in the door like a logjam. I could see Mister Hawkesworth trying feebly to push his way out bum first.

My master didn't join the stampede. Calmly he beckoned to a servant.

'Clear this up, Walter. Jack, help him.'

I righted the inkpot and mopped up the spill with a napkin that had been wrapped round the comfits – also sadly spilt and trampled in the rush. Walter gave me a grateful grin.

'Wait, Miles Hawkesworth!'

The poor man stopped in his tracks at the King's command, fear all over his face. The courtiers had now escaped – and Mister Hawkesworth looked helplessly at the closing doors. The King beckoned to him.

'I have changed my mind,' he said coldly. 'Your new composition will have to wait. I want to perform my music this very afternoon. It is the best I have ever composed and I desire that everyone hear it. So you will bring it to me this instant.' He stared fixedly at the Court Composer. 'You assured me just now that it was finished. Why do you quake, man? Was that a lie?'

'Indeed it was not, Sire,' said Hawkesworth with a gulp. 'Your song is ready.'

'Then don't stand there dithering,' snarled the King. 'Fetch it now!'

And then something happened so small that I wondered if I'd imagined it. Miles didn't flee straightaway as I would have done – he looked over to Cromwell and my master gave him a slight nod.

'Run and do as His Majesty bids, Miles,' he said. 'And afterwards I would be most interested in your old teacher's piece of music.'

I carried on mopping up the ink as I puzzled over this little scene. The King had commanded but I felt that Miles Hawkesworth had sought Cromwell's permission to carry out his order.

It wasn't long before His Majesty grew restless.

'Miles should be back with my composition by now!' he growled. 'Where is he? I could have done the journey to his room and back twice over – even with my bad shoulder.'

85

His angry eyes fell on me. 'Jack Briars, you are the only one who has pleased me today. Go and find Miles and, failing that, find my music. It will be easy for a sharp boy like you. It is a song, "Ode to your Dark Eyes", which I will sing to my lady.' He hummed the first few notes, with a sort of lovesick look in his eyes which I found embarrassing. It was no help to me. I didn't read one word of music.

After asking several times, for I had no idea where Mister Hawkesworth was lodged, I finally found his room on the ground floor.

The sound of banging greeted me as I turned into the corridor I'd been shown. Two workers had upturned a heavy chest and were repairing one of its legs. I stepped over their tools and went up to the door of the chamber.

'Tell Mister Hawkesworth we won't be long, but we have to get this done,' one of the workmen called to me. 'Strict orders.'

'I will if he's there,' I called back.

The man laid down his hammer. 'He certainly is,' he assured me. 'He entered not long ago, tutting at our things lying in his way.'

'They say he's a pernickety man who has to have everything in its place,' said the other, lowering his voice, 'and do you know what he said to us? He said we had to keep quiet because he'd be starting some important work in a little while and he needed silence.'

'Did either of you see him leave his room after that?'
I asked.

'No, because he's in there still, like I said.'

'Are you certain?' I asked.

'We have no doubt of it,' laughed the workman.
'Michael here kept an eye on the door as we were
expecting him to come flying out in a temper.'

'And he didn't,' said Michael.

'Then Mister Hawkesworth must surely be here,' I
said. It seemed to me that he was probably gibbering
in a corner, too scared to come back to the King's
presence.

But a thought scratched at the back of my mind.
I'd seen Cromwell in worried conversation with the
Court Composer. And I remembered Cromwell's keen
interest in the music that had arrived from the old
teacher. Was I right to suspect that Miles Hawkesworth
was involved in something more than composing
ballads for the King?

I knocked at the door and listened. Silence. The
men went back to their hammering. I lifted the latch,
stepped into the chamber and stopped short.

I was astonished at the sight in front of me. The
room looked as if a bear had lumbered through it. The
bed hangings were half ripped from their rail, a chair
was tipped on its side and the music stand had fallen
against the wall, its papers scattered all around. In the
corner lay a broken fiddle.

There was no sign of Miles Hawkesworth.

14

I was certain that the court musician had not left willingly. Someone had forcibly dragged him away. Yet it didn't seem possible. There was no other door but the one I'd come through, and the single window was still firmly latched. It was bewildering. Cat would probably have claimed they'd walked through the wall or some such supernatural flimflam.

But that was it! Cat had given me an idea even though she didn't know it. There must be a hidden passage from this room too. Miles had suspected that someone had been searching in here. The panelling was nothing like the richly carved wood of the other rooms and the wall didn't seem thick enough but I could think of no other answer.

I was just running my hands over the carved oak leaves and acorns on the frieze above the panels when the door flew open and in ran Walter, the servant I'd helped with the mess in the Presence Chamber. I jumped away from the wall.

'The King sent me,' he panted. 'He wants that music now and he's . . . losing patience.'

That seemed a mild way to describe our monarch's mood, but I didn't say anything. It was very unwise to speak ill of the King.

Walter was gazing round open-mouthed at the room. 'Where's Mister Hawkesworth?'

'He's not here,' I said. 'Come on, let's find the King's song.'

But Walter shook his head. 'No good me looking. I can't read. I'll set this place to rights. Mister Hawkesworth lived in a funny way and wouldn't let a servant touch his stuff, but I never thought he'd allow his chamber to get like this. Still, he was a musician, and they can be odd.'

While Walter tidied, I quickly sifted through the scattered papers. None of them had been used. Each was ruled with special lines ready for composition. I'd seen music manuscripts prepared like this at the abbey when the monks were about to write down a new chant.

Boxes stood on the table by the wall. They held pieces of music and they didn't look as if they'd been touched in the struggle. I searched through, looking for 'Ode to your Dark Eyes'. There was no sign of the King's ballad for his lady. I couldn't understand why it should have vanished.

Then I spotted a scroll that had fallen behind one of the boxes. It was sealed. I picked it up.

'Have you found it?' asked Walter hopefully.

'I think so,' I said. 'It's the only one left.'

'Shouldn't you open it to check?' said Walter.

'I daren't. If Mister Hawkesworth has sealed it to present to His Majesty, then it must be His Majesty who opens it.'

Walter followed me back to the Presence Chamber, making sure he stayed well behind. I suppose he thought that I would provide some sort of shield against the King.

I bowed low, quaking inside, and handed the scroll to King Henry.

He tore it from my hand and broke the seal. He opened the scroll. 'By George!' he roared, angrily crushing the parchment in his good hand. 'What is the meaning of this? You have brought me some wretched ballad called "Spring Brings Forth the Lambs".'

'Forgive me, my Liege,' I said, keeping my gaze on the floor. 'Mister Hawkesworth was not there so we had to search for the manuscript. This was all we could find.'

'Miles will pay for this,' bellowed the King, 'if he ever dares show his snivelling face again! What am I to sing to my Lady Anne?' He straightened out the crushed score. 'Am I to resort to sheep?'

He lah-lah-ed a few notes and his face showed disgust. 'What a terrible tune,' he scoffed. 'Hear how only two different notes have been used at the start. It's so repetitive a baby could have written it.' He fixed us all with a scowl. 'I cannot do anything with this. I would never start a love song on a B!'

Master Cromwell and I stood as still as sphinxes while this went on. Not even the King's most favoured minister dared to draw the royal attention. Eventually His Majesty slumped in his chair.

'Leave me,' he commanded. 'And take this discordant rubbish with you. You can put it on the midden heap for all I care.' He thrust 'Spring Brings Forth the Lambs' into Cromwell's hands.

At a nod from Cromwell, I picked up the unsigned papers. 'Bring them to my room,' he ordered. We bowed and began to make our backward exit, Walter leading the way. The King suddenly glared at us again.

'Find Miles Hawkesworth and my song at once!'

The moment we were outside the Presence Chamber, Walter bleated something about other duties and sped off.

Cromwell led the way into his private rooms. I followed, expecting to be sent back to the scribes' office the moment I'd put the papers on his desk.

But once in his chamber, my master went round without a word, lighting candles and throwing another log onto the fire. The shadows danced, adding an air of mystery.

'I have a new task for you,' he said. 'And it's a serious matter.'

Here was my chance to prove myself equal to an important mission. I was certain I was going to learn more of what was troubling him – and I wanted to impress by telling him what I'd already gleaned.

'Is it to do with the song that Mister Hawkesworth's old music teacher sent him?' I asked.

'What do you know of that?' Cromwell's tone was even, but he stared keenly at me.

I told him how I'd interpreted the looks and words that had passed between him and Miles when the manuscript had been delivered.

'I'm guessing that Miles Hawkesworth is not only the Court Composer,' I finished, 'and that his disappearance is important in some way. The delivered manuscript is involved, but I don't know how.'

Cromwell gave a small smile. 'I'm relieved that you don't know everything or you'd have my job, but I salute your powers of observation.' He picked up 'Spring Brings Forth the Lambs'. 'This is the very music. It appears to be a ditty about little lambkins. But there is more to it. What do you say to that?'

'If it were a letter, sir, I'd say it was a message, with a hidden meaning.'

Cromwell nodded. 'Indeed, Jack. And you were right that Miles Hawkesworth is not only the Court Composer. Few people know that he also works for me as part of our . . . network. He is a skilled code maker.'

'So the music *is* a message!' I gasped.

'And it comes from Spain. Miles has a contact . . .'

'You have men in Spain?' I interrupted. 'And in other countries?'

'Of course,' said Cromwell, with a shrug. 'That is the way of the world.'

This network spread further than I'd ever imagined. I was a tiny part of a huge web, with my master as the spider in the centre.

'Miles's contact is known simply as his old music teacher,' Cromwell went on. 'Together they have devised a clever way of hiding messages. They are encoded in musical scores in a way that only the two men are privy to.'

'So without Mister Hawkesworth the information cannot be known,' I murmured.

'But it is vital that we find out,' said Cromwell. 'It contains a name. For some weeks, I have been aware that information about our political alliances and our defences, which we need to keep private, is being sent to the Spanish Court in Toledo.' He sat down heavily in his chair. 'There is a traitor here at Greenwich. A traitor who is playing a dangerous game.'

15

I stared at him. 'Is this to do with Queen Katherine?'
I asked. 'I know the Spanish are unhappy that His
Majesty wishes to replace his queen with Lady Anne
Boleyn.'

'Queen Katherine is one of their own,' said Cromwell,
'and aunt to their king. They are a powerful enemy.'

'And they'd be even more powerful if they had our
secrets,' I gasped.

'I share your horror,' said my master. 'Whoever the
spy is, he is obviously a trusted member of the English
Court. One who fits in without raising suspicion and
all the while is gleaning valuable information. I don't
know how much he has discovered so far but I want it
stopped!'

'How did you find out that this man existed?' I
asked.

'We realised that the Spanish knew more about us

than they should,' said Cromwell. 'Someone here was sending them information.'

'And Miles's "music teacher" has now found out the name of the traitor,' I said eagerly, 'and sent him a warning message encoded in the music. That was the scroll that arrived earlier for Miles Hawkesworth. No wonder he was so keen to work on it!'

'And, as you observed, I was keen to let him,' said Cromwell. He prodded the music with a ringed finger. 'The name we are seeking is in here.'

'How can you be sure?' I asked.

'A good question,' answered my master. He pointed to a small mark on the paper that I would never have noticed. It looked like a hangman's noose. 'This is the agreed sign. But now, when I need Miles's decoding talents more than ever, he has disappeared.'

'Don't you have any clues as to who the traitor might be?' I asked.

'The only thing we know is that he's a courtier,' said Cromwell. 'Aycliffe and another of my men have been looking into this for me.'

I suddenly remembered my winnings stowed inside my livery.

'Is Aycliffe's partner his friend, Francis Shawe?'

'I could deny it but I have a feeling you wouldn't believe me,' said Cromwell. 'They are but two of the many who work for me. It is safer for you and for the country that you don't know the names of the others. If you were ever captured by an enemy . . .'

I heard the warning in his words.

'I'd never give anything away,' I declared. 'Even if I were being tortured.'

'You would if your fingernails were being pulled out,' said Cromwell dryly. 'I believe it is agonising.'

I tried to push the image from my mind.

'So that's why everyone who works for me knows only fragments of the whole business,' Cromwell went on. 'You join a very small band of men who know that Miles is a decoder. You only knew about Aycliffe and now you know about Shawe. But that is all. It is safer that way.'

'And only Mister Aycliffe knows of the special work I do for you?' I asked.

'Exactly,' said Cromwell.

I was beginning to feel rather important. I'd been let into the secret of Miles Hawkesworth's job! 'I thank you, sir, for putting your trust in me, and seeing my value when I have worked for you for so little time. . .'

'Enough of your flowery words, Jack,' my master interrupted. 'It is merely *because* you've been here so little time that I can trust you. And, after all, you are not a courtier.'

I deflated immediately. However, I had no chance to dwell on this as my master was speaking again.

'Miles's disappearance worries me greatly. It happened just after the coded music arrived. I want you to exercise your considerable reasoning powers and tell me what possible explanations you think there could be.'

This made me feel a little better. I was certain that Cromwell had his theories. He was merely testing me. I thought hard. 'If there hadn't been signs of a struggle in the room, I might have thought that Mister Hawkesworth himself was the traitor,' I said. 'The message could have been a warning that he was about to be exposed. It is therefore possible that he left the room in that state to cover his tracks and make us think he was taken. But I still don't think he can be.'

'And why's that?' asked Cromwell.

'If he were the traitor, he'd surely have taken the coded music with him when he disappeared, not the King's manuscript.'

'Good.' Cromwell nodded.

'The answer seems clear,' I said. 'The traitor must have discovered in some underhand way that Mister Hawkesworth was your decoder. He abducted him.'

'But why would the abductor take the King's music?' asked Cromwell.

'He can't have known he had the wrong score,' I said. 'He must have thought he had the message from Spain. Suppose he were in the Presence Chamber when the King first roared at Miles Hawkesworth to go and work on the scroll from "his old music master". The traitor must have known what that really meant. The courtiers were then banished from the room – the traitor among them. He did not hear the King change his mind and call Mister Hawkesworth back.'

'Thus the traitor would hurry to Miles's chamber in order to intercept the coded music,' said Cromwell. 'But why do you think he took Miles too? He would surely only need to destroy it and his secret would be safe.'

'It would be foolish to leave the decoder at liberty to raise the alarm,' I said.

My master gave a grim smile. 'You are thinking like a true spy, Jack. Have you worked out how he carried out the abduction?'

'That is a mystery,' I admitted. I couldn't tell him my theory about the hidden passage. I had promised the King.

'Nevertheless you have done some excellent work, Jack,' said Cromwell. 'You have not disappointed me. We must discover what has happened – and with all speed. That is your task. I want you to start investigating straight away. You may tell Mr Scrope that you are still busy with me.'

'Thank you, sir,' I said. I may have sounded calm but my innards were churning, whether from anticipation or fear, I wasn't sure. Perhaps a bit of both. I'd been given a mission as if I was the likes of Robert Aycliffe.

'Wait!' said Cromwell. 'I'm not telling you to catch the man. Simply find out what you can and come back to me. Tread carefully. If he finds out that you are on his trail, you could be in grave danger. He will be desperate to stay out of our hands. A traitor knows what awaits him if he's caught.'

'Will he be executed?' I asked.

'Not immediately,' Cromwell replied. 'Traitors have valuable information and we always make sure we extract it – one way or another. When they are of no further use – then they die.' He opened the scrolled music and laid it on the table. I itched to look at it and try to unlock the code but I knew I must stick to my orders.

'And now I should be with the King in his Privy Chamber,' my master went on. 'I will be chided for tardiness. We have a meeting with the French Ambassador and he never stops talking. I hope His Majesty will be in a fair mood. I shall study this message later. I may stumble upon the name in it – but Miles and his "old teacher" are fiendishly clever with their codes.'

'Don't you have any other decoders?'

'Of course,' said Cromwell. 'But I do not know which of them I can trust. Our man in Spain sent this information to Miles. That means he knows that Miles is not the traitor.'

I bowed and turned to go.

'Remember, Jack,' said Master Cromwell. 'Find out who has abducted Miles and come to me. No more. And do not speak of it to anyone.'

I bowed again.

Mr Scrope tutted at the news that I was engaged on yet more business for Master Cromwell.

'There is so much copying to be done,' he moaned. 'And you've been off making up riddles and winning bets! Everyone's talking about it.'

Mark grinned but Oswyn ignored me, though I saw his knuckles whiten round his quill.

I couldn't stop the smile spreading over my face. Until that moment, I'd forgotten the riches tied to my belt. So much had happened since I'd won them. But it seemed I'd been the only one to forget. My success had travelled round the palace more quickly than the plague!

'Well done, Jack,' whispered Mark. 'I'm glad you weren't here when Oswyn found out. He turned red as a beetroot. It quite alarmed me because there was a boy once who did that and burst into flames! Don't tell him I told you so, but Oswyn did try to make the King laugh. Apparently he got shouted at for dancing a jig. Not surprising. I saw him practising. I'm glad you won the wager and not him. Well done.'

'Thanks,' I whispered back. 'Sorry I haven't been here, Mister Scrope,' I said loudly. 'It's just that wherever I went, people stopped me and wanted lessons in riddle making. I'm happy to teach any of you . . .'

Oswyn raised his head and fixed me with a glance of hatred. Before he could make any retort I gave him a friendly nod and hurried out of the room. If Weasel-face had known I'd been entrusted with finding a traitor, he'd definitely have burst into flames.

I was going to search the Court Composer's chamber with a fine-tooth comb. There had been signs of a struggle, so it was possible that Miles's abductor had left some clue to his identity.

I dashed down the gatehouse stairs and was striding along the corridor on the ground floor when someone yelled.

'Jack! Wait!'

I knew that voice. I'd bet my newfound wealth that Cat had heard about the riddle and had come to remind me that it had been her idea in the first place. I couldn't have been more wrong.

'Walter's been telling me how the King went into a rage because his music's gone missing,' she exclaimed as she caught up with me. 'I heard you were there as well.'

'What exactly has he told you?' I asked as she followed me along the corridor.

'He said he'd had a terrible ordeal,' said Cat in excitement, 'and His Majesty did all but breathe fire! He said how you both went to Mister Hawkesworth's room to find some music and you took the wrong piece to the King because it was the only one he hadn't put away and it was sealed so you didn't know it was "Spring Brings Forth the Lambs" and not "Ode to your Dark Eyes", but "Ode to your Dark Eyes" was the one he wanted and then he exploded!' She paused for breath. 'Have you been listening to a word I've said?'

I had, and her words had struck fear into me. If Walter was telling the story to all and sundry, then the traitor would be sure to hear and would realise that he had the wrong music. Perhaps I was in time to stop the story spreading too far.

'Has he told anyone else?' I asked.

'Most of the palace by now, I should think!' laughed Cat. 'Is it true the King threw the music at Master Cromwell and told him to stick it on the compost?'

'It is,' I said. 'But I don't suppose the King would want stories about his ill temper passed round . . .'

'I won't tell another soul,' Cat assured me. 'Apart from Mr Wiltshire and the boys in the sewing room.' She headed off before I could stop her.

I wanted to curse out loud. With the story whizzing round Whitehall, the traitor would soon know that not only did he have the wrong music but that the coded message was in Cromwell's hands. My master could be his next target. He might be safe for now, ensconced with the King and the talkative French ambassador, but I would have to warn him the moment he was finished.

I continued on my way. I turned into the corridor outside Mister Hawkesworth's room. It was empty, even of noisy carpenters. And that's probably why I heard it. A soft footfall behind me. I stopped. And a beat later, someone stopped too. There was no reason why they shouldn't be coming the same way as me but why in this furtive manner? I turned quickly. There was no one there but I could see a shadow across the floor, back where the passage turned.

There was no doubt about it. I was being followed.

16

The corridor was quiet – too quiet. I marched past the Court Composer's room and headed for the sound of distant voices. I'd be safer in a crowd. Any wrongdoer was not going to attack me in front of others. He'd be giving himself away.

But more importantly I needed to get sight of this dangerous enemy. As soon as I was round the first corner I peeked back. He was coming out of hiding at the other end of the passage and I got a clear view of his face, although he couldn't see me.

It was Oswyn Drage! *Could he be the traitor?* I wondered. I soon decided that he couldn't – he wasn't good enough at tailing without being spotted. I set off again, whistling as I sauntered along. I had to shake him off, and quickly. I led him up some stairs and along to the door of Lady Tresham's room. I knew it would be empty. Cat had told me that no one would move into that chamber while tales of Duke Humphrey's ghost abounded – and she was making sure that they did abound. I slipped inside and dived into the hidden passage, hoping that if Oswyn had heard the ghost stories too, he wouldn't follow me in.

However, from the click as the door latch lifted, it seemed that Oswyn was not put off by the thought of coming across the dreaded Duke Humphrey. He had another think coming.

I heard him give a gasp of astonishment at seeing the empty room. It was all I could do not to give myself away by laughing as I peered at him through the spyhole.

'You're here somewhere, Jack Briars,' he called, throwing himself into a chair. 'I'm not even going to search for you. I'll wait until you come out, and then I'll know what you're up to.'

'Oh no you won't,' I muttered under my breath.

I let out a low, moaning sigh. Weasel-face sat up. I moaned a little louder. Weasel-face jumped to his feet. 'I know that's you, Briars.' But I was pleased to see he looked worried. 'You've got to show yourself in the end.'

I gave three knocks.

'You can't fool me,' declared Oswyn.

I scratched the panel. Slow menacing scratches as if dead men's nails were clawing their way back from the grave.

'I'm not scared,' called Oswyn, a little less sure this time.

I groaned horribly. Oswyn's eyes grew round as cartwheels and he began to shake.

I let out the most blood-curdling screech I could manage. This was too much for poor Weasel-face.

'Help!' I heard him wail as he stumbled from the room, knocking over a chair in his terror. 'It really is haunted!'

Feeling cramped, I slowly stretched my legs. My foot touched something on the floor. I had no candle so I felt about, and my fingers closed round a heavy ring. I moved my hands all around and discovered a trapdoor!

I grasped the ring and gave it a tug. It didn't move. It couldn't have been used for ages. I tugged again and again until at last I felt a tiny movement. It took all my strength to raise the door, and I coughed as dust flew into the air.

Beneath the trapdoor was a narrow circular stairway. It wasn't as dark as the passage and I realised it was lit by narrow slits in the wall. I knew I should be heading straight to Miles's room, but all my instincts screamed at me to find out where the stairs led. I could hear Brother Matthew's voice in my head. *Are you sure you're not just being nosy, Jack?* Well, yes, I had to admit there was a tiny bit of curiosity driving me on too.

I closed the trapdoor above my head and set off down the stairs. I wondered if the King knew about this secret way. He certainly hadn't used it recently. The trapdoor hadn't been opened for a long time.

I looked through one of the slits. There below me was the inner courtyard. A yeoman was marching across it.

I came to a small landing. Here, the lower part of the curved wall was made of wood and I spotted a tell-tale pinprick of light. There must be a chamber on the other side.

As soon as I looked through I knew where I was. Carefully I slid the door open and stepped into Miles Hawkesworth's room. This door wasn't in the panelling of the outer wall like the others but in the corner where the wall seemed to bow. I hadn't had the chance to inspect that part before I'd been disturbed by Walter.

The light from the room lit up the rough floor of the passage. I saw spots of blood and the scuff marks of a struggle. It looked as if Miles had put up a fight when his abductor tried to drag him through the small door. I was going to follow the steps down. I lit a candle, took the tinderbox just in case the flame went out and slipped back into the wall. The light proved to be essential as there were no more slits and I reckoned I must be underground now.

The stairs came to an end but I wasn't in one of the palace cellars. Instead another passage led away – it went as far as I could make out with my candle. I started along it, ears pricked for any sound. I tried to work out the direction I was taking. The stairs had circled twice and then one quarter more. This meant I was walking away from the river.

We'd only been at Greenwich Palace for a few days, but I'd begun to get an image of its layout in my head. I reasoned I must now be under the Privy Garden. I kept stopping and listening for any sounds ahead, but I only heard my own breathing.

If the traitor had used this tunnel, he was probably far away by now. Part of me hoped this was true because the thought of meeting him in this lonely place where my cries would never be heard scared me. But I wasn't going to stop. This man was willing to betray his King and country. He must be brought to justice.

I reached a small staircase that wound upwards. The tunnel continued beyond it but I couldn't see an end. I checked out the stairway first but I'd hardly climbed a step when the smell of bacon told me I was under the smokehouse. I came to a trapdoor above my head.

I was about to push it open when I heard something below. It sounded like a whimper.

Every nerve was jangling as I crept along the tunnel. I listened hard but now it was eerily silent. I hadn't gone more than twenty paces when a ragged, rasping sound reached my ears. My candle lit a hollowed out cave. Something lay in a heap on the floor. By the light of my flame it looked like a discarded bundle of clothes. But then it moved and gave a pitiful groan. I ran and knelt on the ground, placing my candle beside me.

To my horror, the pale face of Miles Hawkesworth stared up at me. His hair was matted with blood, and dark trickles trailed down his forehead. His hands were bound in front of him. When he saw me his face contorted and his lips moved.

'Tell Cromwell . . . haven't told him . . . anything,' he gasped. His mouth formed one last word. 'Babbage.'

17

Miles Hawkesworth's head fell back, his eyes unseeing. I felt his chest. There was no rise and fall. I didn't want to believe it but there could be no doubt. Cromwell's code maker was dead.

I crouched next to his body, forcing myself to take in the scene. His doublet was open and his shirt ripped. Red, raw marks stood out clearly on his chest. They could only have been made with a flame. The bonds cut cruelly into his hands, and his fingers were twisted into impossible angles.

Miles Hawkesworth had been tortured. I felt sick with horror.

His captor had held a candle flame to his skin. He'd broken every one of his fingers. I couldn't imagine the pain Mister Hawkesworth had suffered. And yet he'd kept quiet.

He'd used his dying breath to tell me that he hadn't

blabbed. And I was willing to bet my silver sixpences that his last word was the name of the traitor.

I couldn't detect any fatal injuries. I looked again at Miles's bloodless face. His lips were dark in the candlelight. Back at the abbey, old Brother Jerome had a weak heart and his lips would turn black at the slightest exertion. Miles must have had a weak heart too. The shock of the torture had been too much for him.

And then it hit me as if I'd walked smack into a wall. The traitor hadn't got the information he wanted so he'd left his victim alive. That could mean only one thing. He intended to come back and finish the job.

I had to get to Cromwell immediately and tell him what I'd discovered – even if I had to burst in on his meeting with the King and the French Ambassador. There might even be time to alert the guards. The King had told me not to talk of secret passages to anyone, but if it meant catching a dangerous traitor . . .

A distant rattling sound made me catch my breath. I remembered Cat's stories of Duke Humphrey.

Then I saw it. A tiny flicker of light further up the tunnel. This was something much worse than a ghost. Miles's murderer was coming back.

I blew out my flame and flattened myself against the wall. A tall figure in a cloak strode up to the entrance of the small cave. I couldn't make out his face in the shadow of his hood, but there was no mistaking what he had in his hand. He carried a heavy chain with a spiked ball on the end. One blow from that would cause such agony that a man would spill all his secrets to make it stop.

He placed the candle on the ground and stood over Miles's body as he wound the end of the chain around his fist. The spikes of the ball glinted in the flame. I was thankful that Miles could no longer feel any pain.

'Are you ready to tell me the code now?' He spoke in a rasping growl. There was silence. The traitor bent over the body.

I heard an angry curse as he realised that his victim was dead. Dead without giving him the vital information.

He stood up and for a brief second the candlelight shone on him. I clamped my hand over my mouth to stop myself crying out.

I could only see a dark cloak and a blank shadow inside the hood. The man had no face!

God's breath! I'd let my fears rule my eyes. His face was simply covered in a kerchief of some sort. Yet, although he'd hidden his features, there must have been something about him that the composer had recognised, for I was certain as I could be that he'd named him.

Silently I crept away. The tunnel curved, cutting me off from his light, and I was plunged into the pitch dark. My shoe caught on something hard and I fell onto the stone steps of the spiral staircase.

The noise echoed down the passage. For a second

nothing happened. Then I heard footsteps and the rattle of the chain. The traitor was coming. I couldn't risk the stairs and the trapdoor. There was no time.

I fumbled in the dark, feeling desperately for a hiding place. My fingers found a small gap behind the bottom steps. I squeezed myself in. I had to bend one arm up against my body and twist my knees almost to breaking. I hoped I couldn't be seen. I prayed I couldn't be seen.

The light of a candle began to flicker round. I drew myself further back. The light swung to and fro and I could hear the links of the chain clinking together. I'd always thought that the hours I'd spent in the abbey chapel were the longest I'd ever endure. I'd been wrong. As the footsteps prowled round the chamber and the beam swept the floor, it felt like my whole twelve years all over again. I was sure that any minute the searcher would find my hideout. He was being very careful. I just hoped he wasn't careful enough.

Now there was silence, as if the man was listening for the slightest sound. I remembered every detail of the treatment he'd given Miles.

I held my breath.

18

At last the light moved away. I managed to turn my head enough to catch sight of a tall figure silhouetted in the beam from his candle before he strode off in the direction of the palace.

I made myself count slowly to a hundred before I decided it was safe to come out. A dead silence had fallen over the tunnel. I slowly extricated myself from under the stairs, trying not to groan as I straightened my cramped legs.

I felt my way to the stairs. I wasn't going to risk taking the same route as the traitor. I climbed up into the smokehouse and ran for the palace.

My news couldn't wait for the French ambassador to stop talking. But as I headed across the Inner Court for the staircase that would take me to the King's Privy Chamber, I heard a weaselly voice.

'Where have you been, Abbey Boy?' Oswyn slipped out of the shadows. 'Shirking as usual.'

God's blood! I didn't have time for this.

'You thought you could fool me with your silly ghost trick this morning.' Oswyn swaggered up to me. He stood so close I could see the bogies up his nose. 'That was unwise,' he went on. 'I'm afraid I'm going to have to speak to Master Cromwell about you . . .'

I didn't hear what he was going to tell Master Cromwell because at that moment there was a shrill cry.

Mrs Pennycod was charging across the courtyard like a small bull. 'Oswyn Drage! Keep away from my Jack!'

'You get old ladies to fight your fights, do you?' sneered Weasel-face.

Mrs Pennycod didn't hesitate. She slung her ladle at him. He turned to flee and it bounced off his bum, leaving a soupy stain on his livery. I counted myself very lucky to have such a fierce protector – with such a good aim. She might be an old lady, barely as tall as my shoulder, but Oswyn had scarpered.

'Thank you,' I said, bending and kissing her cheek.

'Get on with you!' she laughed, flapping her apron at me. 'I was just stirring the potage when I saw that fiend out of the window.'

I retrieved her ladle. 'It's a bit bent,' I said.

'It's not the first time,' she said. 'This dent is from when that cheeky article in the dairy stuck his tongue out at me. And the bent handle is from when Tom the log boy put spiders in my shoes!'

'Well, I'm very grateful to you and your ladle,' I told her.

She shrieked with laughter and scurried back to the stillroom. I dashed for the stairs. As I made my way up to the first floor I had to dodge through the flood of people spilling out of the Presence Chamber from luncheon. It chilled me to think that Babbage the traitor could be one of them, laughing and joking with his courtier friends as if nothing had happened. And he'd soon be finding out something of great importance to him. He'd soon know that Thomas Cromwell had taken the coded music away. My master would not be safe.

At last I burst from the crowd and dashed for the King's rooms. The gallery that Mark had told me about stretched along the front of the palace. Through the windows I could see the river. A servant was sweeping the landing stage steps, two boatmen were hailing each other and a grand barge was setting off into the current. Life was going on as normal. Little did anyone guess that behind these walls, a dangerous traitor was threatening the safety of the country.

A yeoman guard stood at two massive golden doors. He watched me skidding to a halt and his halberd twitched in his hands. The urge to burst in on the King abruptly left me. I forced myself to behave in a dignified fashion.

'Good afternoon, sir,' I panted, giving a slight bow. 'I have an urgent message for Master Cromwell.'

'Then you're in the wrong place!' said the guard, when he realised I was harmless. 'He's heading upstream as we speak.'

I stared at him. 'But I . . .' I mumbled, my thoughts racing.

This was the last thing I'd been expecting. Cromwell must have been on the barge I'd seen leaving. I wondered where he could be going at such a difficult time.

'He's with the King,' said the yeoman. 'The Duke of Suffolk came not twenty minutes ago and swept them off for some river air. They won't be back for hours.'

I thanked him, cursing the King's brother-in-law. Though I was sure the rest of the Court would be grateful that their grumpy monarch was out for a while.

'I'll tell Master Cromwell that you came haring after him as if the world was coming to an end,' the yeoman said with a smile.

'Oh, no, please don't,' I said quickly, suddenly fearing that it might get to the ears of the wrong person. 'My message can keep. Mister Scrope said I had to say it was urgent, but it's only about . . . er . . . ordering some new quills.'

'So you were just trying your luck,' laughed the guard. 'You'd have looked a bit foolish if I'd let you in!'

I took my leave, walking calmly away though I wanted to hit the walls in frustration. It came to me that perhaps I should tell Robert Aycliffe, but I dismissed the thought at once. Cromwell had set Aycliffe and Shawe to work together, but he had been clear that I was to work alone and tell no one. It was up to me. At least the traitor must be feeling safe at the moment. He had no idea that Mister Hawkesworth had given anything away before he died. And my master was safe too for the time being, out there on the Duke's barge.

I would carry on with my investigation. I thought about my one clue – Babbage – the name of the traitor. Cromwell had said that he knew the man was a courtier. I'd go back to the office. There was sure to be some list or other of all the people at Court.

But as I approached the gatehouse, Oswyn appeared in the doorway. He looked as if he could barely contain his fury at being chased away by Mrs Pennycod.

'I've been waiting for you,' he said, planting himself in my path. 'I want you to know that your days here are numbered. I'll make sure of it.'

'Oh yes?' I countered. 'And how are you going to do that?'

'You'll just have to wait and find out,' replied Oswyn. 'But I know you're up to something.'

I was suddenly drenched in cold sweat. Had Oswyn found out about my special work for Master Cromwell? How had I let this happen?

'I don't know what you mean,' I said, trying to sound unconcerned.

'Don't play the innocent with me,' snarled Oswyn.

'You've been disappearing from the office with a different excuse each time.'

'I've been busy,' I said. 'It takes a lot of effort to make His Majesty laugh and win a purseful of coins.'

'You always think you have a clever answer,' he spat. 'And as for your winnings – you didn't get them without an underhand trick or two. But what can we expect from an abbey foundling? You're nothing but a cheat.' He shoved me in the chest, sending me reeling backwards.

I'd heard men speak of anger causing a red mist that blinded them to anything else. Now I knew what they meant. I leapt on Oswyn and knocked him to the ground.

19

Before I could land the first blow my fist was caught in an iron grip. I was hauled off Oswyn and spun round. I found myself confronting Robert Aycliffe. He looked furious.

Oswyn stood up, brushing himself down and shaking his head as if I was a simpleton who didn't know any better. There was almost a smile on his lips.

I tried to struggle free. I was going to beat him to a pulp.

'Stop that!' growled Aycliffe. I ignored him but he clouted me round the ear. For a second I saw stars.

'What happened?' asked Shawe.

'I wish I knew,' said Oswyn coolly. 'He attacked me. I have no idea why.'

I wanted to shout, 'He started it!' like a child but I knew I had to swallow my rage. That was almost impossible while Weasel-face was standing there knowing he'd made me look a fool.

'Get back to your work,' Francis Shawe told Oswyn. 'We'll deal with Briars.'

'He's not to be trusted,' said Oswyn. 'If you ask me, he should be dismissed.'

'But we're not asking you,' said Aycliffe coldly. 'Go.'

Oswyn bowed. 'I'm happy to leave it to you gentlemen to sort it out.' He turned on his heel. As he sauntered away he suddenly bent down, picked something up and stashed it in his shirt. I wondered if it was a stone to throw at me later.

'Oswyn's got it in for me,' I tried to explain as soon as he'd gone. 'I wanted to teach him a lesson once and for all.'

If I thought they were going to pat me on the back and agree that Oswyn was nothing but a maggot-ridden weasel who deserved all he got, I was wrong.

Aycliffe looked down at me sternly. 'I never expected to find you brawling like a common urchin,' he said. 'What would Master Cromwell think if he knew? You have a *responsible* job with him, after all.'

I knew he didn't only mean the scribing. But he couldn't say more in front of his friend. A little worm of shame began to burrow into my heart. Aycliffe was right. I had lost control. The thought of my master getting to hear about it struck cold terror into my veins.

'I'm sorry,' I muttered. 'But Oswyn's trying to get me blamed for things I haven't done.'

'It is the hardest thing to be falsely accused,' said Aycliffe solemnly, 'but sometimes we have to bear the injustice in silence. You're not a child any more, Jack. Yet you behaved like one. I will not say anything about it this time but I cannot promise to keep quiet if it happens again.'

He left me feeling relieved but utterly wretched. Francis Shawe began to follow him. Then he turned with a twinkle in his eye. 'I understand why you wanted to thump Drage,' he whispered. 'He's a little rat.'

Then he was gone, catching up with Aycliffe and slapping him on the back.

I had great respect for Robert Aycliffe and he was right about how I'd behaved. But Francis Shawe was more human. He remembered what it was like to be young and headstrong.

Mister Scrope glanced up as I entered the office. 'I hope Master Cromwell has finished with you for the moment,' he said irritably. 'You've been gone an age and the work is stacking up here.'

'Never mind, Mister Scrope,' said Oswyn, barely concealing a smile. 'You won't have to worry about Jack Briars for much longer.'

Inside I was boiling with anger. Furious with Oswyn and raging at Aycliffe who hadn't let me punch Weasel-face! I couldn't help myself. I had to get a little scrap of revenge.

'Oswyn's right,' I said, coolly. 'Master Cromwell has finished with me . . .'

'What a shame,' Oswyn murmured, enjoying his moment of triumph.

Mark looked pale with horror.

'. . . for the time being,' I added. 'So I can catch up with all the work I've missed!'

Oswyn's hand jerked uncontrollably and splattered ink all over his parchment. Then he gave me a strange smile. 'You must be feeling very pleased with yourself. But I think you'll find I've won in the end.'

I decided not to tell Weasel-face what a bad loser he was.

Mister Scrope thrust a paper at me. 'The accounts for the wine cellar. Two copies for our records and be quick about it.'

I joined Mark at the table. It seemed to me that a large amount of wine had been guzzled in the short time we'd been in Greenwich.

'Tot up the flagons of Burgundy when you've finished, Jack,' called Mister Scrope. 'His Majesty has a taste for it and the Steward's boy can't count the fingers of his own hand.'

I copied the words and numbers of my first task without thinking about them. My mind was on tracking down Babbage.

I leaned over to Mark.

'If you needed the name of a courtier, how would you go about it?' I whispered, too low for Weasel-face to hear.

Mark put down his quill. 'Why do you want to

know?' he whispered back. 'I hope you haven't got yourself into trouble with one of them. It wouldn't be the first time!'

'It's not that,' I assured him quickly. 'I wish I could tell you, but I can't.'

Mark held up his hands. 'Then say no more.'

He nodded over to a large chest in the corner. 'The scroll of courtiers housed at the King's palaces is usually kept in there,' he said. 'Mister Scrope has copies of all the Lord Chamberlain's household accounts and other business—'

'I'll take a look,' I interrupted. 'Thanks.'

'But you won't find it there,' Mark went on.

'Why not?'

'It's being altered, on account of Sir Rowland and Lady Tresham leaving. It will be altered to note their new accommodation.'

'So it's not only a list of courtiers actually sleeping at the palace?' I asked.

'Oh no,' said Mark helpfully. 'It shows everyone who's in attendance. It's a very useful document. You can find out all sorts of things if you read it. For instance . . .'

'I shan't find out anything if you don't tell me where it is!' I said, trying not to feel impatient.

'Ah, yes, of course,' said Mark with a chuckle. 'It's practically under your nose. Well, Oswyn's. He's working on it this very moment. But you'd better wait till he's finished.'

My heart sank. If Weasel-face got wind of the fact that I wanted the list, he'd make sure it didn't come my way for hours.

20

I was going to have to be cunning if I was going to get that list from Oswyn.

Mark stared at me and put his head in his hands. 'Oh dear,' he groaned. 'I'm beginning to recognise that look. You're up to something. You know Oswyn's desperate for a reason to get rid of you. Please be careful.'

'I will – as long as you go along with whatever I say.'

Mark gave a reluctant nod.

'Oswyn!' I called loudly, making Weasel-face jump in his seat. 'We need your help.'

'You think you're going to get help after . . .' he stopped.

'After what?' I asked, trying to look innocent.

'Nothing,' Oswyn said quickly. I could imagine what was going on inside his head. He must be boiling mad that I'd escaped dismissal. 'What is it?' he growled.

'I have a wager with Mark,' I answered. 'I bet him

I could think of five courtiers whose names sound like vegetables. He said I couldn't. Loser has to pay a forfeit.'

Mark looked bewildered. I winked at him, hoping he'd join in with the pretence.

'You won't win this bet, Briars,' snorted Oswyn.

'But I only need one more,' I pleaded. 'You've got the Court accommodation list. Would you check Cabbage for me? I'm sure I heard of someone the other day. . .'

A sly smile spread over Oswyn's face. I realised there was a flaw in my plan. If by some incredible chance there was a Cabbage at Court he wouldn't be in a hurry to tell me. He was going to make sure I lost and I'd never get the chance to check for Babbage.

I sauntered round and peered over his shoulder as he ran his finger down all the names beginning with 'C'.

'Nothing,' he declared.

'Try Babbage then.' I pretended to sound annoyed. 'That's close enough. That would be all right, wouldn't it, Mark?'

Mark nodded slowly.

'It's cheating, more like,' muttered Oswyn. 'You shouldn't have agreed to that, Mark.' He pulled out another page. 'As I said,' he sneered when we'd both examined it, 'you lose.'

I went back to my seat and patted Mark on the back. 'You were right after all,' I told him. 'Now I have to paint my face blue, stand on one leg and cluck like a chicken. That was the bet, wasn't it?'

Mark gulped. 'I'm glad *I* didn't lose,' he said faintly.

Good old Mark. I was beginning to realise how much I could rely on him.

'I'm surprised you're not giving him some of your winnings,' said Oswyn smoothly.

'Mark knows I'll share with him,' I replied. My hand went to my belt. The purse was gone. I only needed one glance at the mocking look on Oswyn's face to know that he'd got it. It must have fallen during the fight – and that was what I'd seen him snatch up. And I could prove nothing.

I forced myself to smile. 'We'll sort it out later, Mark,' I said. 'But for now I must do some work.'

I went back to counting my wine flagons and forced myself to forget the purse. I had something much more important to deal with. Finding the traitor. No courtier had the name Babbage. But there might be a servant with that name. Someone who had done the dirty deed for a courtier. The palace was full of servants – another daunting task. But surely their names were written down somewhere.

'Mark,' I said coaxingly.

He looked up.

'If I wanted to know the name of a servant . . .'

'How would you go about it?' he finished for me. He sighed. 'First courtiers, now servants. I *really* don't want to know what you're up to.'

'But you'll help me?'

He nodded. 'The Clerk of the Board of the Greencloth would keep such a list.'

'Then I'll go and see him right away,' I declared.

Mark looked shocked. 'He's much too important!'

'You're forgetting,' I teased him. 'I'm the boy who made the King laugh when no one else could. I'm sure I can get round this Clerk.'

'Don't even think of it!' breathed Mark. 'You won't be allowed near him.'

'But if he's the one with the list . . .' I began.

'There's an office run by his deputies,' said Mark. 'They may have copies but why you should want . . .' He broke off. 'No, don't tell me. It would only cause me worry, I'm sure. They have an office on the ground floor, directly across the Inner Court from here, second door on the left, past the tapestry showing the story of Abraham and Isaac.'

'Thanks, Mark,' I said. 'You're a good friend.'

He brightened.

I stood up and flapped the wine cellar accounts. 'These figures don't make sense, Mister Scrope,' I said. 'I'd better go down to the cellars and ask someone.'

The Chief Scribe scowled at me suspiciously.

'We don't want to run the risk of not ordering enough,' I said. 'It might upset the King.'

'Go!' squeaked Mister Scrope in alarm.

∽♪∼

The door of the deputies' office was open. I poked my head in. A man was tying ribbon around a scroll. Luckily he wore royal livery which showed he was a servant like me. I didn't think any of the highborn deputies would want to help a lowly scribe.

'I've been sent by Lady Tresham,' I said.

I'd decided to take a leaf out of Cat's book and name someone who wouldn't be questioned about the matter. In Lady Tresham's case this would work for two reasons. She wasn't housed in the palace now and she was far too scary to approach!

'And what does her ladyship want?' asked the man.

'There was someone here at Greenwich who did a small job for her,' I explained, hoping he wouldn't ask what it was. 'And she would like to reward him. His name is Babbage.'

The man's eyes twinkled. 'Are you sure that's who she said?'

'I'm certain,' I replied.

'I do know one of that name,' said the servant, a huge smile on his face.

'And where will I find him?' I asked, eagerly.

'He'll be waiting for you.' The man seemed barely able to hold his laughter in. 'He lies in the graveyard at St Alfege's Church. Old Barnaby Babbage has been dead for years!'

'Then that cannot be the man she was thinking of,' I said, forcing myself to grin in a pretence that I'd enjoyed his joke. 'I'll go and ask her again.'

'Rather you than me!' said the servant, turning back to his task.

I thanked him politely for his help and left.

My thoughts were turning faster than a spinning wheel. There was no living Babbage at Court. How could that be? Unless it was a false name that someone was using. And would I ever find out who that was?

All the time the traitor was at large, my master was in danger. He could be back from his river trip by now. I would have to warn him that the traitor knew that he had the music.

But when I knocked on his office door, there was no answer.

'Hello, Jack!' It was Cat. 'What's wrong? You look as if you've got the troubles of the world on your shoulders. You should be the happiest boy in the palace after winning that money.'

'I haven't got it any more,' I told her. I explained what had happened, though I was too worried to feel more than a brief spike of anger towards Weasel-face.

'I'll stick pins in that Oswyn when I get hold of him!' she said vehemently. Then she peered hard at me. 'But that's not what's worrying you, is it?'

'There's nothing wrong with me.'

'I know you're telling fibs,' she said. 'Tell me exactly what's going on or I'll stick pins in *you*!'

'I'll take that risk.' I forced a laugh.

She planted herself in front of me. 'Come on, Jack. We're friends, aren't we? I think you need help.'

Her face was serious. I was torn in two. I didn't want to involve her in this terrible business but I knew I could do with her help. Then it dawned on me that she probably wouldn't let me go without knowing all! I'd bravely told Cromwell that I would never let out secrets, even under torture, but torture was nothing compared with Cat Thimblebee!

I made sure that no one was in earshot. 'I have a . . . mission,' I whispered.

'Count me in,' exclaimed Cat eagerly.

'Don't be so sure,' I said. 'This is deadly.'

'Lord have mercy!' breathed Cat. 'Are you in danger?'

I didn't answer that.

'I'm on the trail of a traitor,' I said.

Her eyes grew round as I explained about the coded music. They grew even rounder when I described the underground tunnel and the grisly discovery of Miles Hawkesworth. She crossed herself and muttered a prayer.

'I feel really mean now for calling him fussy,' she said.

'We'll make sure he didn't die in vain,' I said and then told her the dead man's last words. 'But now I have this impossible task of finding Babbage.'

'Babbage?' she declared. 'Are you sure that's what he said?'

'That's just what the man in the deputies' office asked,' I sighed. 'Don't bother to tell me about Barnaby Babbage in the graveyard.'

'I wouldn't dream of it,' said Cat. 'I know a Babbage who's very much alive. You should have come to me right away. I'll take you to him.'

I gasped. 'Where is he?'

'Follow me.'

Cat set off, taking a staircase down, and heading past the kitchen.

'Wait,' I said, catching her arm. 'We must be careful. If I'm right, he's a killer.'

'Oh, he's that all right,' said Cat. 'But he'll be having a meal and we'll be safe while he's eating.' She led the way out into a small stone yard. I followed nervously, casting my eyes around for a vicious murderer. But the only thing in sight was a large tabby devouring a fish head.

'Babbage,' said Cat, squatting down next to it, 'may I introduce Jack Briars? Jack, this is Babbage. He belonged to Mister Hawkesworth.'

She burst into laughter. I began to scowl but then I saw the funny side too. Miles had been concerned for his pet. That's why his last word had been his name.

'He's not your murderer,' said Cat. 'It's only the mice that have to worry about him. And I'm not sure even they will soon. Mrs Pennycod has adopted him. He's been eating so much fish and pigeon pie he'll never look at another rodent!'

21

Cat promised that she'd let me know if she came across any traitors. I told her to keep well away from anyone who looked suspicious.

'I'd have to keep away from you then!' she called over her shoulder as she trotted off down the passageway.

I tried the King's Privy Chamber again. The same guard was on duty.

'I haven't seen them come back,' he told me helpfully. 'I'll warrant the Duke is going to dine somewhere with him and the King.'

The courtyard clock struck five. I hadn't realised it was so late. I was supposed to be back in the office and if I was away much longer I'd be working half the night. It was beginning to get dark when I entered.

'You've been gone an age,' grumbled Mister Scrope, looking up. 'I hope you've got the figures.'

I'd forgotten all about the flagons I was meant to be

counting. 'Yes, sir,' I said. 'I'll finish the wine account now.'

My fingers might have been busy with my quill but my mind was a million miles away. I had to know where Master Cromwell was – and that he was safe. Supposing my master *had* come back and the guard simply hadn't seen him. Suppose he'd gone to his room to find the traitor there, waiting for him. A good spy wouldn't just sit copying accounts. He'd be off, scouring the palace to find his master. But how could I possibly get away again?

I jumped as the door swung open. Thomas Cromwell himself walked into the room. I nearly fell off my seat in relief.

'Ah, Mister Scrope,' he said. 'I've some extra work to be done and as young Jack took time off to make riddles with the King he can come and do it now while the rest of you go to supper.'

Mark looked alarmed. I imagined he was worried about me missing another meal.

Cromwell didn't speak until we were in his office and the door was shut.

'I hope you have news for me,' he said.

'It's the worst news, sir,' I answered. 'Mister Hawkesworth is dead – and your life is at risk.'

Cromwell sat down heavily in his chair. 'I feared for him,' he said, ignoring the news of his own peril. 'Tell me everything you know.'

'I found him dying,' I told him, hoping he wouldn't

ask where. My promise to the King was nearly slipping from my tongue. 'I think we were right, sir. The traitor must have thought that Mister Hawkesworth was working on the coded music. He kidnapped him from his room and when he realised it was the wrong piece, he tortured him to find out where the real one was.'

I expected my master to react with the same horror that I'd felt. If he felt anything, he didn't show it.

'He gave me a message for you,' I went on. 'He said "Tell Cromwell I haven't told him anything".'

A flicker of hope flashed across Master Cromwell's face. 'Was there more?'

I hesitated. 'He gave me a name.'

'The traitor's?'

'So I thought,' I said. 'It turned out to be the name of Hawkesworth's cat.'

Cromwell slammed a fist on the table. 'Damn Miles!' he growled. 'He thought more of that mangy animal than of any living person.' He wiped his forehead. 'If we cannot find this man, England is in grave danger.'

I stood quietly, fearful that we were standing on the edge of an abyss. The room was silent.

'And my danger?' he asked at last.

'The gossip flew round the palace about the King having the wrong music. The traitor will now know that you have the coded message.'

Cromwell's expression was impassive. Not a flicker of fear showed.

'I guessed as much,' he said, 'for this chamber has been searched.'

I looked around the tidy room. 'How can you tell?' I blurted out.

'I have several . . . shall we say . . . markers round the place,' he said. 'They have moved.'

I realised how little I knew about Cromwell's secret world and the risks he ran every day.

'And the music, sir?' I asked.

Cromwell reached into his robe. There seemed to be a hidden pocket. He pulled out the scroll. 'It has been with me the whole time. Tell me, Jack, does anyone else know about Miles's death?'

'They cannot,' I said. I didn't need to mention Cat.

'How can you be so sure?' My master was looking at me in that way he had. He knew I was keeping something from him. 'Where is the body?'

I'd been foolish to think he wouldn't ask. Perhaps there was a way of keeping my promise to the King and telling Cromwell what he needed to know.

'If this were a story told to a child . . .' I began.

'I don't want tales, Jack,' said Cromwell. 'Speak plainly.'

'But if it were,' I persisted, 'the villain would know of a hidden passage that led from the palace. A passage that would allow him to kidnap his enemy, kill him and leave the body where no one would ever find it.'

'You're telling me there's a secret way out of Greenwich?' demanded my master.

'I'm merely telling you a story, sir,' I said. 'A story in which a royal magpie also knows a little of this passage and has commanded that it be kept secret.'

For a brief instant, I saw astonishment on his face. 'That would be a tall tale indeed,' he said slowly.

'And in that tale, unbeknown to the traitor, a boy would come upon the dying man and hear his last words.'

Cromwell nodded. Now I knew that he'd understood and wouldn't push me for more details about the tunnel. 'The traitor must not find out that you spoke to Miles before he died.'

'If he did he might flee from the palace,' I agreed. I pushed away the thought that he might also want to kill me. 'Then it would be even harder to track him down.'

'And he must be tracked down,' said Cromwell grimly.

I thought of what happened to traitors. Weeks of 'persuasion' in the Tower to get information out of them, followed by the slow, terrible death of being hanged, drawn and quartered.

Cromwell picked up the scroll. 'I believed this safe while I had it,' he said. 'But obviously that is not the case now that all and sundry know it is in my possession. Take it and hide it somewhere. The traitor would never expect me to give such an important document to a mere scribe.'

I felt as if I was holding a viper! This flimsy piece

of music hid the key to England's safety and would reveal the traitor. It could strike and bite me at any moment.

I looked at the squiggles and lines. 'It will disappear until you can find a way to decode it,' I promised.

Cromwell sighed. 'And when that will be, I have no notion. Miles and his contact worked out the code between them. All he ever said was that "the key is at the start".' He rubbed his forehead as if he had a pain there. 'But every piece of music has a key signature at the beginning.'

'Perhaps I can help,' I said. 'Brother Matthew often set me puzzles and coded challenges.'

My master smiled. 'I will remember that and call upon you if I need you.'

I had the feeling that he thought I had little hope of success. And deep down I knew he was right. But that wouldn't stop me trying – if I got the chance.

'I want you to do nothing more than hide the music,' said Cromwell, as if he'd read my thoughts. 'You must leave the rest to me.'

'But what about your safety?' I asked.

'That also you can leave to me.' He gave me a small smile. 'But thank you for your concern.'

I opened out the music and went to tuck it under my jerkin.

'No, that is too risky,' said Cromwell. He pushed a box towards me. It had his gold initials on it. 'Put it in here.' He hesitated and replaced it with a plain one from a shelf. 'This will serve you better. It has no association with me. Stay out of danger, Jack.'

I nodded. I hoped I would with all my heart.

I slipped out of the room when no one was passing. As I made my way back to the scribes' office, I thought up and discarded a million hiding places. I had to decide soon. Carrying the scroll about was too perilous. It chilled me to think that someone could be following me now. Someone who knew too much. Someone who was waiting for a chance to get his hands on the coded message.

Someone who didn't care how he did it.

The passageways were busy with servants heading to the Great Hall for supper. I was going to miss another meal. But this time I couldn't spare my stomach a thought.

I pushed against the tide and ran to the sewing room. Mister Wiltshire was just telling everyone to pack up and head for their food.

'Excuse me,' I said. 'Master Cromwell asked if someone could mend his . . . erm . . .'

I couldn't think of anything!

'That will be the hem of his cloak again,' said Cat quickly in a tone that brooked no argument. 'He keeps catching his foot in it. I'll see to it, Mister Wiltshire.'

And she'd gathered up her tools and pushed me out of the room before anyone could say a word.

'What's going on?' she whispered eagerly as she led me down some stairs and into the dairy. She checked it was empty and closed the door behind her. We crouched down between the cheeses. 'And what's in that box?'

'The coded message,' I told her.

'You shouldn't be carrying it around!' gasped Cat, jumping up and leaning on the door as if she thought that would keep the traitor out. 'It's too dangerous to have that thing on you.'

'Which is why I've come to you,' I said. 'I need you to find a really good place to hide it. I have to finish some work or I'll be in trouble.'

'I know the very place,' Cat declared. 'And the sooner I do it the better. I'll hide it in Lady Tresham's bedroom. No one will sleep in there on account of the ghost story.' She gave a triumphant laugh. 'I'll sew it into the bed curtains. They're lined, you see, so there'll be a space.'

'But the traitor might see the stitching,' I said.

'How dare you!' said Cat, sounding highly offended. 'My stitches are invisible. In fact they're the best in the palace. That scoundrel will never find it.'

She took the box from me, holding it out as if she thought it might explode. 'And then I'll put word about that the ghost has actually been seen in the room,' she said. 'I defy the bravest in the land to go near the place after that!'

I didn't think that would stop a determined villain but I couldn't think of a better plan.

Cat poked her head out of the door, and crept off,

glancing left and right in a very exaggerated manner. Any traitor would have spotted her a mile off, she looked so suspicious. Though they'd probably have kept away from her, thinking she was mad!

I rushed back to the scribes' room and got on with the wine account, ignoring my growling stomach. Without warning the door swung open and I leapt to my feet, ready to fight off an intruder. But it was only Oswyn and Mark back from supper and ready for bed. I realised I was getting as jumpy as Cat with her ghost stories. But with a traitorous murderer on the loose I reckoned I had a much better reason to be nervous!

We laid out our blankets on the floor of the office – as usual I was furthest from the fire – and I vowed to wake early. When I got the chance I would go to Lady Tresham's chamber and take a look at the music. I was never beaten by Brother Matthew's puzzles, which were sometimes very tricky, and I wasn't going to be beaten by this one. I pushed away the thought that I might fail.

ঔ

I did wake early but it wasn't quite how I expected. I was deep in a dream where I was galloping on Diablo's back towards a dark castle when suddenly I was wrenched out of the saddle. I woke to find a hand clamped over my mouth.

22

Someone pulled me to my feet. I was about to kick out but the dagger pressed into my neck soon made me decide against it. I found myself forced out of the room and onto the empty landing. One small candle flickered in the sconce, casting a shadowy light.

I felt a blast of cold air from an open casement window.

'Don't make a sound, Jack.' The voice was husky and close to my ear. I didn't recognise it. All I could tell was that this was a man – and tall. It was also someone who knew me – and perhaps even knew what I'd been up to. I tried to swallow down my fear.

'Scream for help and I'll cut your throat!' The knife pressed in deeper. Slowly my mouth was released. But now my captor grabbed my arm and twisted it painfully up behind my back. He pushed me forward until I was pressed against the window ledge.

'I have a job for you, Jack,' the husky voice said in my ear. 'I need a piece of music.'

The cold air was nothing to the ice flowing in my veins. I was in the hands of the traitor. I told myself I must stay calm. It was my opportunity to discover this man's identity – if I lived to reveal it.

I had to make him believe that I knew nothing about the coded music. I tried to think myself into the mind of an ordinary scribe, woken from sleep, who had not the first idea what was going on.

'Who are you?' I stammered.

He shook me. 'You don't need to know that. It is the music that's important.'

'What music?' I whimpered.

'A piece that was mistaken for the King's composition,' came the answer.

'King's composition?' I repeated, trying to sound bleary and bewildered.

I was rewarded with a clout around the head and a violent shaking that wrenched my bent arm.

'Don't act the fool, Jack! Everyone at Court must have heard about it. His Majesty was given the wrong music this morning in the Presence Chamber. He gave it to Master Cromwell and told him to get rid of it.'

'Then I expect Master Cromwell obeyed the King,' I tried.

'I am certain that he did no such thing. All you have to do is agree to a simple task and you'll be left alone.'

I racked my brains to place his voice. The husky

growl gave me no clues. I needed to turn to see his face, but his iron grip told me I had no chance of that.

'What do I have to do?' I muttered.

'That's better. I warrant the music is still with Master Cromwell. I want you to get it for me.'

'How can I?' I said. 'I don't know where he put it.'

His answer was to press the knife back to my throat. 'If you value your life, you'll find it. I've heard that you were with Master Cromwell when he took it from the Presence Chamber. You went with him to his rooms, I think.'

'I expect it'll be there then,' I said, trying to sound hopeful.

'It is not,' was the answer through gritted teeth. 'But you will find it.' I felt a sharp pain and something warm trickled down my neck.

'You won't get away with killing me!' I said hotly. 'Master Cromwell doesn't like his scribes being stabbed to death.'

'I have no intention of stabbing you. It's too messy,' the low voice went on, sending a new wave of fear through me. 'There'll be blood everywhere and tell-tale wounds on your body. Everyone will know you've been murdered.' His tone was still husky and unrecognisable but now he sounded as if we were having a friendly conversation. 'No, you will merely have walked in your sleep and had an unfortunate fall and in a week's time the tragic foundling will be forgotten. Let me show you.'

He pressed me down so I was half lying over the window ledge, my toes barely touching the floor. I stared at the distant ground, my heart hammering. A stone pavement lay beneath me. He released my bent arm. Pain shot through me as I tried to straighten it.

'The guards will come by any minute,' I gasped breathlessly.

'Do you think I'm stupid, Jack?' sneered the man. 'They've not long made their patrol, and will not return until the quarter hour. No, I have long minutes to tip you over and be gone.'

I began to shiver in the cold air. At least, I tried to tell myself it was the chilly night and not sheer terror. I heard the clock striking in the Inner Court. He was right about the time. It was eleven and the guards wouldn't be back until a quarter past. My fingers found a stone carving. I gripped it, although I knew it wouldn't stop me falling.

'Not a pleasant thought, eh, Jack, being splattered all over the flagstones?' He thrust me further out, one hand gripping me round the back of the neck. 'But it needn't happen if you find the music for me. You're a bright boy. You'll find a way.'

It was all I could do to stop myself blabbing that I knew where the music was. I had to do as my master would – I had to tell myself that my danger was nothing compared with the danger to England if the coded message fell into this man's hands and his identity was never revealed. But I wasn't sure I was brave enough to die for my country. I felt the hard stone under my hand and gripped it more firmly. I felt it move! A small flicker of hope rose inside me. If I could work the stone loose I'd have a weapon.

'I don't want to help you,' I said like an obstinate child. 'Why do you need the music anyway?'

'Merely to destroy it,' said my captor. 'The tune is not . . . to my taste.'

The stone shifted under my hand. It would come loose at any second. I would throw it behind me. I could see it striking him in the face. When he fell back, I'd run for my life, shouting at the top of my voice.

'This is your last chance,' my captor growled in my ear. He was gripping my throat so tightly I could hardly breathe. 'Agree to find it or you are dead.'

The stone came loose from the wall. I had it in my grasp. In a single movement, too quickly for him to react, I slung it over my shoulder. I heard a window pane shatter and felt shards of glass falling on me. The stone tumbled past my ear and down into the courtyard. It had missed him completely and hit the closed window beside him. My one chance and I'd failed.

But the man let out an angry oath. Footsteps were coming from the scribes' room. In desperation I scrabbled for a shard of glass and gouged the hand that still held me. My captor cursed with pain and snatched his hand back.

'You're not getting away with this!' he hissed into my ear. 'Fetch the music and leave it in Miles

Hawkesworth's room. Then your life will be spared. You have till midnight. An hour should be more than enough.'

I was about to tell him that was the last thing I was going to do, no matter what he threatened, when he spoke again.

'And if you don't do exactly as I say, I will seek you out and slit your throat!'

23

With a vicious twist of my arm, he was gone.

I lay over the sill for a moment, not quite believing I was still alive. Then hot fury flooded through me. The traitor had no mercy. He was ready to kill anyone who stood in his path – even someone he thought to be an innocent scribe.

Well, I would fetch the music. But not until I'd done all I could to prise out its hidden message. If I failed, then I knew with dread what my next move would have to be. I'd have no choice but to let the traitor take the music. I didn't want to die and it wouldn't help my master or my country if my throat was slit. But that couldn't be the end of it. I'd follow him and find a way to get the music back and expose him, whatever the danger.

I was just easing my way back in through the open casement when I heard Mark calling to me. He peered through the door of our office, his eyes wide with fright.

'Are you all right?' he gasped. 'I heard glass shattering. And you've cut your neck! What happened?'

Of course I couldn't tell him. But my captor had given me an idea. I pulled my face into a dazed expression.

'Where am I?' I muttered. I looked about wildly, then let my eyes focus on Mark and gave a huge yawn. 'Oh hullo, Mark. I think I've been sleepwalking.'

'God's breath!' whimpered Mark, rushing to my side. 'This is terrible. I woke you up while you were sleepwalking. They say you must never do that. I'm so sorry, Jack. It means you could die!'

Mark had no idea how right he was, although my possible death would have nothing to do with sleepwalking!

'Don't worry,' I told him. 'I was already awake.'

Mark looked relieved. 'Do you remember anything?' he asked. 'Was it you who broke the window?'

'Window?' I looked vaguely around, and started as if I'd only just seen the fragments of glass at my feet. 'Yes, I must have.'

'I won't tell anyone,' he said, guiding me back to our room. 'And no one will know we were here.'

'Good idea,' I said.

He came to a sudden halt. 'You could have fallen to your death!'

'I'm sure I'd have woken up before that,' I said.

For some reason Mark didn't seem convinced.

While we crept back into our chamber he muttered about sleepwalkers who'd tumbled down stairs, fallen into fires and drowned in buckets. Oswyn snorted and turned over but he didn't wake. He had something clutched in his hand. I was sure it was my winnings and my fingers itched to reclaim them, but I didn't have time to worry about that now. It must be at least quarter past now. I ran through my plan as I waited impatiently for Mark to fall asleep.

It wouldn't be easy to get to Lady Tresham's room. I'd have to be sure that my attacker wasn't following. And once there, I'd need to cut the stitches in the bed curtain. I'd get a quill trimming knife and . . . God's oath! That wouldn't work – Oswyn was pressed right up against the chest where they were kept. I'd never get it open without rousing him. I'd have to wake Cat and borrow her scissors. She could at least tell Cromwell the truth if the traitor caught up with me and my dead body was discovered.

I reckoned the traitor would be waiting for me to leave the room. He'd follow me and kill me the moment I had the music in my hand. If I was to outwit him, my only means of escape was through the window. I thought back to Oswyn shouting at me from that very window when I'd been in the courtyard the day before. There wasn't a trace of ivy on that wall. I'd have to risk that I could still get down to the ground.

Mark was asleep, at last. I pulled on my livery jacket and crept to the window.

I slowly opened the clasp, wincing at the sound of scraping metal. Behind me, Mark didn't stir and Oswyn just snored loudly. I climbed onto the sill and closed the window. But the bricks below were too smooth for footholds. On one side the wall came to a corner, which was carved with a zigzag pattern all the way to the ground. Perfect for my escape – and hopelessly out of reach. Or was it? I looked up. A narrow ledge ran right across above my head. Hoping that the patrolling guards wouldn't suddenly appear, I stretched up and hooked my fingers over it. It took my weight. I inched my way along, legs dangling, to the corner. My fingers were throbbing by the time I began my descent. I didn't know what excuse I'd make if the guards came upon me clinging to the walls in the middle of the night. They'd never believe I'd been sleepwalking, and I could hardly say my cap had blown off again!

As my feet touched the ground, footsteps rang out on the flagstones. There was nowhere to hide.

'Halt, who goes there?'

Two guards came running up, halberds held out ready to stick into me. I was caught against the wall. *Damn the devil!* I thought. If the traitor hears this commotion he'll know I'm out and about.

'I'm Jack Briars,' I said, putting on a wobbly voice. At least I like to think I was only playacting my fear. 'I'm one of the scribes.'

152

'And what is a scribe doing out at this time of night?' demanded the nearer, a man with wide shoulders and muscles to match.

'Mister Scrope,' I bleated, making it up on the spot. 'He . . . um . . . demanded some food . . .'

One of the guards looked doubtful. 'A likely tale,' he scoffed. 'You're after a feast for yourself. Get you gone back to bed!'

The other guard laughed. 'Don't be hard on the boy, Philip. Don't you remember waking with a terrible hunger on you at his age?'

'I admit it,' I said, holding up my hands. 'I missed supper tonight and I shan't sleep if I don't get something to stop my belly growling.' I put on my most woebegone expression. 'I only wanted a crust of bread.'

'Go on then,' said the cheerful yeoman. 'But don't let anyone see you or you could be in trouble!'

Little did he know how true that was! I thanked him and headed straight across the courtyard to the kitchen. I slid into the shadows to wait, trying not to think about bread, or any other kind of food for that matter. As soon as the two men were out of sight I slipped off to the workroom where Mister Wiltshire's staff were sleeping.

I picked my way round the dark room and gave Cat a nudge. She woke with a start.

'I need your scissors,' I whispered in her ear, before she'd had a chance to scream.

Cat sat bolt upright. 'Why?' she whispered back. 'You're not thinking of taking over my job, are you? I can tell you now, you won't . . .'

'I've got to get the music out from the curtain where you stitched it.'

Cat said nothing, but stood up, took her apron and led me out of the room, into a corridor where there were no sleepers.

'What's all this about?' she demanded. 'I've only just hidden it.'

'And now I have to get it, try to decode it and raise the alarm if I manage to discover the name. And all before midnight!' I exclaimed.

I quickly told her about my sinister visitor. 'And if I can't work out the name I'll have to go after him and try to stop him myself.'

'You're not going anywhere near that madman,' exclaimed Cat. 'I'm coming with you to make sure you don't.'

'No, it's too dangerous.'

'If you think I'm going to stay there and let you be murdered then you're madder than a . . . mad person!' She tied her apron round her waist in a determined manner that reminded me of Mrs Pennycod at her fiercest. 'Anyway, you'll only ruin that curtain.'

We argued back and forth. Then a smug look came into her eyes.

'You'll never decode that message without my help!'

I had little hope of finding the secret of the code so

how she thought she could help me when she couldn't read or write, I had no idea. But it looked as if she was coming no matter what I said.

We crept along the corridors, stepping over sleeping servants and jumping at every sound. A nearby clock showed half past eleven. Time was running out.

24

We reached Lady Tresham's room. I listened at the door. Silence. I lifted the latch and went inside. A pale light from the torches in the Inner Court below came through the window. I made for the bed.

Then I realised that Cat was still hovering at the threshold.

'Come on,' I hissed.

She didn't move. 'Duke Humphrey could be hiding somewhere, ready to jump out with his slit throat gaping and blood spurting everywhere.'

'There is no ghost in this chamber,' I told her. 'You just told everyone there was, to keep them all away from here.'

'I know,' she replied. 'But everything's different at night.' Reluctantly she stepped inside, gazing fearfully around her.

I decided there was only one way to take Cat's mind off her worries.

'Give me the scissors. I'll cut the music out,' I said cheerfully. It worked. I knew she wouldn't let me touch her precious stitching.

'You're not going near that curtain,' she declared, pushing me aside and beginning to cut the thread carefully. At last I pushed my fingers inside the lining and retrieved the manuscript.

'What's that writing say then?' asked Cat.

'Sweet lambkins gambol in the spring,' I read. 'Hey nonny nonny no. Yuck! This is as stupid as the King's love song, but don't tell him I said that!'

'And how is that a code?' asked Cat. 'Unless it's a code to make you throw up!'

I thought hard. 'I remember Master Cromwell talking about what he knew,' I muttered. 'It wasn't much . . . he told me that Miles Hawkesworth said there's always a key at the beginning.'

Cat stared at the parchment. 'I don't see a picture of a key. In fact, there are no drawings at all.'

'Maybe he meant the key that unlocks the code,' I said.

'That's as clear as mud,' said Cat. 'Any other clues?'

I was imagining the hands on the courtyard clock moving round relentlessly to midnight. And I had to have this decoded and find the guards to arrest the traitor before then. The task seemed impossible. I forced myself to think.

157

'The King complained about this being a baby tune opening with only a couple of different notes,' I said.

'Well, it's not meant to be a great piece of music, is it?' said Cat. 'It's pretending to be. In here somewhere is a clever coded message for a spy.'

I looked up at her, a thrill running through my body. 'Brilliant, Cat!' I exclaimed.

'Eh?' Cat looked confused.

'The tune doesn't matter. The notes themselves hide the code!' I put my finger on the first note. 'That's a B,' I said.

'How do you know?' demanded Cat. 'Can you read music?'

'No,' I said. 'His Majesty told me, in a way. He bellowed that he'd never start a love song on a B, like this one!'

'So what's the next one?' asked Cat eagerly.

'The names of the notes follow the alphabet. Brother Matthew tried to make me take an interest in music at the abbey but he didn't get very far. Now I wish I'd listened. Anyway, if this first one is a B, and the next is one note below then that must be an A. Then there's two more Bs and another A. Now there's a different note.' I carefully counted the lines and spaces on the stave. 'That must be a G and the next one is . . .' I couldn't believe what I was looking at. 'I've got it!'

'Well I haven't,' said Cat crossly. 'You know I can't read. What does it say?'

'It says Babbage!'

'All that shows is that Mister Hawkesworth was obsessed with his moggy!' snorted Cat. 'It doesn't get us anywhere at all!'

'Oh yes it does,' I told her. 'The last word Miles said was Babbage. I thought he was telling me to look after his cat but that wasn't it. And he wasn't telling me the name of the traitor either. He didn't know the name – because he hadn't had the chance to look at this, and also because his murderer's face was hidden. He was telling me the key to the code!' I stared hard at the manuscript in front of me. 'Brother Matthew and I were always sending hidden messages to each other – but I can't think how this one works.'

'What sort of codes did you use?' asked Cat.

'The first one he taught me was the letters of the alphabet written out on one line and underneath he put the alphabet backwards,' I said. 'So if I saw an A in my message, I knew that meant Z, and a B was Y and so on.'

'That sounds impossible to me,' said Cat ruefully. 'I wouldn't know an A from a Z.'

'And this one's even harder,' I said. 'I can't work out how the code helps to decipher the message.'

'Is Babbage written again?' asked Cat.

'No it's not,' I said impatiently. 'There's plenty of Bs and As and Gs and Es in the music but they're not all together.'

All at once I felt as if I'd been searching for a tiny

needle in the hugest haystack and found it had been stuck in my finger all the time.

'It's all to do with the letters in Babbage!' I declared. 'We look for the next B note and see what letter of the song is directly underneath it. Look, that's a *b* too. Then the next note A . . . that's over a letter *e* . . . yes, I'm sure that's how to decipher it but we've got no quill and paper to write down what we find.'

'Typical scribe!' scoffed Cat. 'You think you can't write at all if you can't do your beautiful curly letters all over a fine piece of parchment.'

'Well what do you suggest then?' I asked crossly.

'We've got charcoal from the fire and we've got the floor!'

'Ah yes – I suppose that will do.' She'd got the better of me – but this wasn't the moment to dwell on it.

Cat peered out at the courtyard clock.

'We've only got fifteen minutes!' breathed Cat. 'This is taking too long.'

I quickly looked along the notes for the next B – the third letter in Babbage. Directly underneath, in the words of the song, was a letter *w*. I carried on, writing down the letters I found. Babbage seemed to be repeated seven times. It was slow work, but eventually I got to the end of the piece. Once I'd separated the letters into words, a strange rhyme stretched out along the wooden floorboards.

'What does it say?' demanded Cat. 'Is it the traitor's name?'

'No,' I said. 'It reads "Beware one high by the sea. 'Tis certain who does treachery".'

'Is that it?' said Cat, disappointed. 'It's not much help.'

'But it must have meant something to Miles Hawkesworth,' I insisted. 'The answer's right at our feet, if we could just think of it. It looks as if it's a code within a code. These words must have another meaning. Beware "one high by the sea". Think, Cat, what's high by the sea? I've never seen the sea.'

'Nor have I,' said Cat, 'but I've heard there are waves on the sea that can be high and I've heard of a high tide.'

'Maybe it means someone who comes from the sea,' I wondered. 'Someone from a foreign land like Spain – but it doesn't help with a name.' I looked at her in despair. 'We're never going to raise the alarm before midnight,' I said. 'There's only one thing we can do now.'

'What's that?' asked Cat.

'Put the music in the room for the traitor to take.'

'We can't let him get away!' exclaimed Cat.

'We won't,' I said grimly. 'I'm going after him.'

'You could get yourself killed.' Cat sounded horrified.

'When I agreed to take on this special work for Cromwell I knew it might be dangerous,' I said. 'My master left me in no doubt of it. He also made me understand that my King and country must always come before my life. I've made my choice.'

Cat rubbed out the charcoal words. 'I've made my choice too,' she said simply. 'I'm coming with you.'

25

We crept down the quiet corridors and stopped at the door of Miles Hawkesworth's chamber.

'We'll hide inside,' I whispered to Cat. 'The traitor's bound to use the secret passage – for his own safety.'

'Not a good idea,' Cat whispered back.

'Why not?' I asked.

'If he finds us in there we're as good as dead.'

'But if we stay out here, we'll have no way of knowing when he takes the music. We might not hear anything to alert us.'

'That's easily solved,' said Cat. She pulled a length of thread from her apron pocket. 'When you put the music in there, tie this to the sliding panel of the hidden passage, stretch it across the floor and under the chamber door, but so that it's hidden from his view.'

'So when the sliding panel moves, the thread

moves and we know he's come in to get the music,' I exclaimed. 'That's clever!'

'I know it is,' said Cat smugly. 'One more thing – you'd better make sure the thread is tied to the very bottom of the sliding panel – find a loose bit of wood or something to attach it to.'

'Why?' I asked.

'Because, you clodpole, if you tie it higher up, the traitor will fall over it as he steps into the room.'

I had to admit she was right – as usual.

I quickly slipped into Miles Hawkesworth's chamber. Light from the torches in the Inner Court filtered in here too so it wasn't completely dark. I picked my way to the music stand and left the parchment there. My fingers felt along the panelling until they touched the sliding panel to the hidden passage. I searched the bottom of it and found a carved acorn. My desperation made me fumble and drop the thread. I took a deep breath and tried again until I was sure I'd tied the end of the thin thread to it, knowing all the time that a cold-hearted murderer could be just the other side of the wall. At last the thread was secure. I trailed it behind the table, well away from the music stand, and across the floor towards the chamber door.

I joined Cat. We sat in the dark, both holding the end of the thread. She nudged me and pushed some bread into my hand. It was very welcome!

'If only we could have solved the rhyme,' I whispered

as I chewed. I repeated the words. 'Beware one high by the sea. 'Tis certain who does treachery.'

'Sam in the sewing room used to live in Dover till he came to the palace,' said Cat. 'He told me that's by the sea. It sounded like a very strange place. There's the land – and then a big drop down to the water. He called it something. A cluff? A clift? No. What was it? That's right, he said it was called a cliff.'

'We're not getting anywhere,' I groaned. 'And it must be nearly midnight. Wait a minute – are you sure he said a cliff?'

'I think that's what it was called.'

'And it's high by the sea?'

Cat nodded.

'Then I think we've got the name,' I said slowly.

Cat looked at me in amazement. I felt sick to my stomach.

'The rhyme says beware one high by the sea. A *cliff* is high and it's by the sea. . .' I gulped. 'A cliff . . . Aycliffe . . . Robert Aycliffe is the traitor.'

We stared at each other for long moments. My mouth had said the words but it couldn't be true.

Cat echoed my thoughts. 'Mister Aycliffe a traitor! I can't believe it. He's always been so kind to me – and generous too. Only last week he gave me an extra penny for mending his riding breeches. Who'd have thought he was more than just a lawyer.'

'He's much more than that,' I said bitterly. 'He's one of Master Cromwell's men – like me. A trusted spy.'

I felt a violent surge of resentment against the man who'd tricked us all so well. 'Of course that's how he's got away with his double dealing – by acting the generous courtier, so that everyone would think well of him and no one would suspect him.'

I remembered his recent cold behaviour to me. Had I caught a glimpse of the real Aycliffe – callous and cruel?

'He has no loyalty to England!' I exclaimed furiously. 'He's willing to betray King and country – and probably gets well paid for his trouble.' I hesitated. 'But how could he have been the same man who threatened to send me to my death last night? His voice was nothing like Robert Aycliffe's.'

The truth was, I wanted to believe that we'd got it wrong.

'Simple.' Cat shrugged. 'He disguised it. You've told me you've done it yourself when you didn't want to be found out.'

I stood up. Somewhere a clock struck twelve.

'What are you doing?' gasped Cat.

'I'm going to get the music back and take it to Cromwell,' I said. 'He can decide how to proceed against Aycliffe.'

I didn't add that I also wanted to get Cat away from danger. I'd just reached for the door handle when the end of the thread jerked and was pulled from my hand.

Cat stifled a gasp. 'Too late.'

26

We sat in the dark corridor, straining our ears for the slightest sound. I grabbed the thread again waiting for its next movement.

'He's a real expert,' I whispered. 'He's made no sound to give himself away.'

'But he's not as expert as we are,' Cat whispered back. 'He can't have found my thread or he'd have been out here like an arrow.'

'If only I'd found the answer sooner,' I muttered. 'We'd have had time to alert the guards and Robert Aycliffe would have been under arrest by now.'

'Don't blame yourself,' Cat hissed. 'We know where the tunnel goes. As soon as we're sure he's scarpered, we'll raise the alarm. The guards will find him, you'll see.'

I shook my head. 'Aycliffe is too clever to let himself be caught. He's probably got a horse waiting for him.'

The thread twitched again.

'He's gone.' I jumped up and seized the door latch.

'What are you doing?' demanded Cat.

'I'm going after him.'

Cat caught my arm. 'No, Jack. It's too dangerous. You've done all you can.'

I shook her off. 'There's no time to argue. We're the only ones who know the traitor's identity. I'd never forgive myself if he gets away.' I opened the door and crept into the dark room.

'The music's gone,' I said, pointing to the empty stand.

We tiptoed over to the hidden panel.

'I can't hear anything,' whispered Cat, her ear to the wood.

I slid open the secret door. It was dark, but we couldn't risk a candle.

'Are you sure you want to do this?' I asked Cat.

She nodded grimly.

I led the way down the stairs. The slits in the wall let in a dim light from the torches outside. But when we reached the tunnel it was black as night. Cat grabbed my arm.

'There he is,' she hissed.

His candle flickered faintly in the distance. And as soon as we'd seen it, it was gone.

'Has he put it out?' came Cat's voice in my ear.

I shook my head and then realised she couldn't see

that. 'The passage bends,' I told her, 'and he's moving faster than we are.'

'Easy for him,' muttered Cat.

I felt her clutch the back of my jacket. We edged our way along the cold, damp wall of the tunnel. The darkness was almost solid. It seemed to press on my face like a heavy cloak. We'd only gone a few paces when Cat pulled me to a halt.

'Aycliffe could be waiting for us ahead,' she breathed in my ear, 'and we wouldn't know until it was too late!'

Her fright forced me to keep down my own fear. 'We might not be able to see him,' I said, 'but he can't see us either. Anyway, there are two of us – plus your scissors.'

'You're right,' Cat whispered fiercely. 'And I'll use them if I have to!'

We crept on. The sudden glow of a candle ahead made us shrink back into the dark.

Then it was gone. By its brief light I'd seen that the traitor had passed the steps to the smokehouse. I had no idea how much further the tunnel went – or where it led. But we had to follow.

The tunnel smelt of damp earth. And now there was something else mixed with it – a sweet, decaying odour that turned my stomach.

Miles hadn't laid there long and the tunnel was cold, though nothing could stop Death when it took hold. Now I was very grateful that we didn't have a candle. Cat wouldn't have to set eyes on a rotting corpse.

I took slow hesitant steps. Cat suddenly let go of my jacket.

'Are you all right?' I asked.

'I'm feeling my way along the wall,' said Cat. 'It's safer.'

I was about to warn her that there was a cave ahead and that she would have no wall to guide her when I heard her stumble.

'Cat!' I hissed.

'I'm here.' Her voice was tiny and there was something else. A cold, terrified horror.

'Lord help me, Jack,' she whimpered. 'I've fallen into a grave.'

I reached out and found her shoulders. They were shaking. I pulled her to her feet and hugged her firmly.

'That's Mister Hawkesworth's body, isn't it?' she murmured. 'I was that frightened about Aycliffe hearing us that I didn't think of it. It felt so horrible. He's cold and . . .' She sobbed some more, stifling the sound in my jerkin. Then I felt her lift her head. 'Let's go.' Although it was a whisper, I could hear the determination in her voice. 'I want to catch his murderer.'

I took her hand and we began our faltering way again. We'd not gone more than a few stumbling steps when the ground began to slope upwards.

'Now where are we?' asked Cat.

'I have no idea,' I said. 'Under the Thames for all we know.'

'I hope not,' said Cat, with a feeble laugh. 'I can't swim.'

Our footsteps suddenly sounded louder. 'We're on flagstones,' I murmured.

My groping hands felt a wall in front of us. We nearly walked right into it!

'Have we come all this way for a dead end?' whispered Cat.

'That can't be possible,' I whispered back. 'Aycliffe's not here – so he must have gone somewhere.'

I moved along the wall, willing my eyes to see something in the total darkness.

'I've found a way out!' I whispered as my hands touched rough stone steps hewn into the wall. 'I'm going up.' I hesitated, thinking about what could be waiting for me at the top. 'You stay here, Cat. At least one of us will be safe – and you can go for help if I don't come back. Lend me your scissors.'

I heard a faint snort from Cat. 'Never! Me and my scissors are coming with you.' She gave me a shove. 'Off you go.'

The stone stairs wound upwards and now the darkness was broken by a faint gleam.

'We've reached a trapdoor,' I told Cat, 'and it's open.' I crouched below the opening and listened, Cat by my side. There was no sound from above.

I dared to raise my head above the opening. I could just make out that we were inside a large bare cellar. Beside the trapdoor stood a wooden ladder and a faint light glowed from the floor above.

I led the way cautiously up the ladder and into an empty stone room with glazed windows in each wall. Moonlight through the windows showed a flight of wooden stairs leading to the next floor. I looked back at Cat. Her face was pale. Whether it was fear or the faint light I couldn't tell.

'Where now?' she breathed.

There was no sound of footsteps. The man could be anywhere. Or he could have gone. Then we heard a distant shout of anger. I recognised Aycliffe's voice.

'That came from above,' I whispered. 'Follow me.'

I crept towards the stairs, picking my way round the rushes on the floor. They hadn't been changed for a while. As I put my foot on the first step I heard deep voices. Two men were arguing although I couldn't hear the words. I turned to see if Cat had heard them too. But Cat wasn't behind me. She was standing as if frozen, staring out of one of the windows.

'Do you know where we are?' she hissed.

'No,' I replied, 'but that's not important now. We've got to . . .'

'I can see the palace below,' came Cat's terrified whisper. 'This is where we came for your riding lesson, Jack. And there's the beacon! We're in Duke Humphrey's Tower!' She looked round wildly. 'His ghost could appear any minute.'

I took her firmly by the arm. I could feel her shaking. 'We've got worse things to worry about than an old ghost,' I said. 'Aycliffe is upstairs – and there's someone with him.'

She stared at me for a moment. 'Then we need to go up there too.'

The stairs wound up to the next storey. We took them, treading softly. I expected the wood to creak and alert Aycliffe we were on our way but they were new and well built.

There was a single door at the top and we could hear low voices on the other side.

'What are they saying?' Cat said in my ear.

We inched closer.

A sudden burst of shouting had us leaping back from the door. Almost immediately a clash of sword blades rang out through the air. More followed. A duel of some sort was being played out in that chamber.

I eased the door open a crack – and shut it again quickly. I couldn't quite believe what I'd seen.

'It's Francis Shawe in there fighting with Robert Aycliffe,' I told Cat. 'Cromwell told me he was working with Aycliffe, trying to find clues about the traitor. Shawe must have discovered that his trusted friend is betraying his country!'

'Mister Shawe is a good sort,' whispered Cat. 'Surely Aycliffe won't try to kill him?'

I thought back to when Aycliffe had threatened my life, holding me out over the courtyard. 'I wouldn't bet on that,' I said. 'He's a desperate traitor. Who knows to what depths he'll sink.'

'Then what are we going to do?' asked Cat.

'*You're* going for help,' I told her.

It was a good plan, I thought to myself. We needed reinforcements and it would take her out of harm's way.

'But . . .' Cat began.

'Get Master Cromwell to send guards up here,' I told her. 'Go now!'

'But I can't leave you on your own,' Cat protested.

'No arguing,' I said. 'You've got no choice. You know the palace better than me. You know where the guards are. And I'm not going to do anything stupid.'

She lifted her chin defiantly and for a second I thought she was going to stand her ground. Then she turned and disappeared down the stairs.

The fight inside the chamber was sounding more desperate. I'd been lying to Cat. I was about to do something very stupid.

I flung open the door and rushed in, realising too late that I should have insisted on having Cat's scissors.

'Stop in the name of the King!' I yelled.

Aycliffe and Shawe were in the middle of the room, their swords crossed. Both whirled round at my intrusion and if the scene hadn't been so grim, I might have laughed at the surprise on their faces.

Aycliffe recovered first. He flashed his arm, and with a clang, knocked Shawe's sword from his hand.

Aycliffe launched himself forwards, grasped his friend round the neck and pressed him against the wall, the tip of his blade to Shawe's throat.

27

'Help me, Jack,' said Shawe hoarsely. 'This man has betrayed his country and he means to kill me.'

'You liar!' growled Aycliffe. 'I don't know why you're here, Jack, but you must go to Cromwell at once and tell him that I have caught the traitor.'

I looked at both men for an instant. Each was asking for my help but only one was telling the truth and sadly I had enough evidence to know which one.

Shawe's sword was lying in the corner where it had fallen. I snatched it up.

'Let Mister Shawe go,' I said. I tried not to let my voice crack but I felt full of sorrow and betrayal. 'I will kill you where you stand, Robert Aycliffe, if you don't do as I say.'

Aycliffe's head jerked round and he glared at me. 'You think that I'm the traitor . . .' He broke off and gave a bitter laugh. 'I can't blame you for getting it wrong.' He tightened his grip and Shawe's eyes bulged as he struggled to breathe. 'I thought Francis here was my loyal friend. How mistaken was I!'

What an actor! I remembered his remark about my playacting as he held me over the deadly drop to the Inner Court. I felt like commending his performance now. 'Let him go,' I repeated, raising the sword and pressing the tip into his back.

My voice sounded cold and dead, even to my ears. I hoped it was convincing. I was counting on it. I had never once in my life used a sword and I hoped I wouldn't have to now.

Aycliffe didn't move. A thought jumped into my head. *Why hadn't he killed Shawe the moment he had the chance? Was there still a shred of decency in him that made him hesitate to kill his friend?*

But before I had time to think any more about it, Aycliffe released Shawe and let his sword drop to the floor.

I lowered my blade and looked round for something we could use to tie Aycliffe up.

'Die, traitor!' came a cry. Francis Shawe snatched up Aycliffe's weapon and lunged at him.

Aycliffe tried to twist away, gave an anguished cry and fell to the ground. He lay unmoving. I stared at him in horror and disbelief, still unable to take in that this man we'd all trusted could be such a villain.

'Thank you for believing me, Jack,' said Shawe. 'You saved my life and saved England from a vile traitor.

How lucky that you came here.' He wiped his bloodied sword on Aycliffe's doublet and his expression changed. He eyed me suspiciously. 'But what is one of Master Cromwell's scribes doing in such a place in the middle of the night? Come, lad. Speak. I think you know more than you are letting on.'

I wished I could tell him the truth, but I knew very well that I mustn't divulge anything. Shawe did not yet have any idea that I worked for Cromwell in the same way he did. Thanks to Cat, an excuse came to me.

'I'd heard stories about the ghost that's said to haunt this tower,' I said. 'I wanted to find out if they were true. I thought I might meet Duke Humphrey. I never thought I'd come across a traitor being dispatched.'

As I said it, Cromwell's words shot through my brain like an arrow. He'd told me that a traitor would never be killed straight away.

'You're just the sort of boy to go ghost hunting,' said Shawe, rubbing his throat where Aycliffe's fingers had grasped. 'And I'm glad for it.'

I nodded but my thoughts were racing. Villain though he was, Aycliffe should not have been run through so swiftly! He might have given some useful information if he could have been persuaded to talk.

'Should I fetch the guard?' I asked. I couldn't tell him that Cat had already gone to do that very thing. He'd find out my real part in all this later – if Master

Cromwell decided to let him know that I was more than just a scribe.

'We'll both go to the palace,' said Francis Shawe, looking out of the window. 'Aycliffe won't be going anywhere.'

He spoke in an icy tone. He must be feeling the betrayal of their friendship as well as of the country. Was that why he had killed Aycliffe outright? To save him from torture? A sort of last kind act? No, there was something about this picture that wasn't right.

Feverishly I tried to recall the coded message. Had Cat and I got the meaning wrong? Was there another way to understand it? A traitor killed on the spot, by one of Cromwell's spies – a man who should have known he must be kept alive. How did the words go again? *Beware one high by the sea, 'tis certain who does treachery.* The message seemed clear. It had warned against Aycliffe – *one high by the sea.*

Brother Matthew's advice jumped into my head – about looking at a problem sideways. And now I could see another way to read the words. *Beware one high by the sea* – supposing that wasn't a warning about Aycliffe. Supposing it was a warning *for* Aycliffe.

That would change the rest of the meaning. *'Tis certain who does treachery.*

Perhaps I'd been wrong to think that the code within a code only applied to Aycliffe's name. There could be one more hidden name there. 'Certain' was another way of saying *sure* – and Shawe was the man standing in front of me!

Was it possible that the coder was warning Robert Aycliffe to beware? *Beware Aycliffe. 'Tis Shawe who does treachery.* But why would he warn Aycliffe? He should be warning everyone – King and country! Then I remembered. Aycliffe and Shawe were working together on this mission. Aycliffe would be telling his friend Shawe all that he discovered. The coder must have known this – and known that Robert Aycliffe would be in immediate danger.

I tried to slow my breathing. I knew I must appear normal. If Shawe was the traitor he mustn't sense my suspicions. There was only one way to find out the truth. In all that had happened, I'd forgotten the coded music. The real traitor would have it in his possession. There had been no time to destroy it.

The candle sputtered. Shawe turned to tend to it and I took the chance to kneel by Aycliffe's body and feel in his bloody clothing.

'What are you doing?' Francis Shawe was striding towards me, the candle in his hand.

'I'm checking that Aycliffe is really dead,' I replied. My heart hammered in my chest. I'd found no sign of the music.

'He's dead all right,' said Shawe. He brought the candle close and held it over the body. 'And all traitors should meet his fate.'

His hand was lit briefly by the light of the flame.

I started as I saw a deep scratch, new and raw. I'd scratched my captor's hand when I'd struggled with him at the open window.

A wave of horror flooded through me. I'd helped to kill a good, innocent man.

I looked up from the scratch and into Shawe's face. He was staring at me with a look that chilled my blood. I realised immediately that I'd given myself away. He knew I'd seen the tell-tale mark on his hand.

Francis Shawe slowly placed the candle back in its sconce.

He drew his sword. 'Stand up,' he ordered. 'You can stop your playacting now. You've found me out.'

Shaking, I got to my feet.

Shawe held the sword at my heart. 'You've been a bit too clever, Jack Briars. I'm afraid I'm going to have to kill you.'

28

I cast about for a way to escape. But my back was pressed against the wall. He'd skewer me before I'd moved a muscle.

'You're a boy of many talents,' Shawe said. 'I could have used you. And you'd have been well paid. What a shame!'

I strained for the sound of the guards approaching. There was silence.

All I could do was try to keep him talking.

'How can you explain away two murders?' I asked. 'It won't be easy.'

Shawe flicked the sword point to my throat, forcing my chin up. 'Are you daring to doubt my intelligence?' he asked coldly. 'I will explain that my good friend, Robert Aycliffe, lured me here to kill me. And then he turned on a poor scribe whose only crime was to go ghost hunting.' He gave a grim laugh. 'I will tell a fine story about how you didn't die in vain because you distracted Aycliffe long enough for me to defend myself. Neither of you will be able to say any different.'

He pulled out the scroll from his jerkin. 'Thank you for delivering this to me so efficiently.'

He held it to the candle. I watched, hope draining as my only evidence burned before my eyes.

Then his sword flashed in the air and I felt its point pressing into my chest again.

I had to stay alive. Of course, I wanted to for my own sake but Cromwell had to know the truth. *Hurry up with the guard, Cat,* I thought desperately. Then I had an idea. I had nothing to lose.

'You don't want to kill me,' I said.

'Oh I think I do,' said Shawe, 'but pray do tell me why not. It will be entertaining.'

'Because, as you say, I could be useful to you,' I said.

I hoped I sounded desperate enough to make such an offer. An offer that might keep him intrigued long enough for the guards to get to us.

'Go on,' prompted Shawe.

'I hear many things at work,' I went on. 'No one would suspect a scribe of finding out more than he should, or of . . . passing it on.' That was truer than he knew!

I caught a tiny movement of the door. Shawe had his back to it. I held my gaze on his face, willing him not to turn around. I made certain my expression gave nothing away but I was thinking furiously. Cat would have told the guards that Aycliffe was the traitor. What would they think when they saw this scene? I doubted I could convince them of the truth before Shawe got in with his story. But for the moment I had to keep on with my pretence.

'In time I might become as skilled as you,' I said earnestly. Francis Shawe looked as if he was considering my suggestion.

The candlelight showed a solitary figure creeping in. I forced myself not to let my eyes leave Shawe's face but I could see that it was Cat – and she was alone. I couldn't understand it. There was no sign of the yeomen guard. Cat caught sight of Aycliffe's body and gave a start. I hoped she'd realise that we'd got the wrong villain. Why else would Francis Shawe have his sword at my throat?

'I wouldn't ask much by way of pay,' I gabbled on. 'In fact I'd do it for nothing. You see, I'm fed up with copying boring old documents. What do you say? Is it a deal?'

'I don't have to make bargains with the likes of you!' spat Shawe. He stopped, a look of stunned surprise on his face.

'There are two swords at your back,' came Cat's voice from behind him. She was trying to sound gruffer and deeper. 'I don't know why you're threatening my friend like that but I'm not having it. Drop your weapon or I'll run you through.'

Shawe lowered his blade and for a second I thought

her strategy had worked. But the next instant, he'd whipped round, his sword ready to strike.

'What the devil?' he gasped at the sight of the small seamstress who was even now holding out her open scissors in a defiant pose. In a flash the scissors had gone spinning across the room and Shawe had his arm tightly round Cat's neck. 'Now, Jack,' he said, pointing his sword at me. 'Do you want to gamble for your freedom? You can try and make your escape while I snap this one's neck or I can let her go and run you through instead?'

'Don't listen to him,' croaked Cat, struggling in his grasp. 'Just run!'

I knew I should do as she said. Only by making a getaway could I hope to have Shawe caught and brought to justice. But I couldn't be the cold-hearted spy. I couldn't leave Cat at the mercy of this madman.

'Let her go, Shawe,' I said as calmly as I could. 'I'm the one you want.'

But as I spoke I heard a faint crackling outside. Flickering light sent shadows dancing across the tower room.

'What's going on?' demanded Shawe fiercely.

I knew perfectly well. Cat must have lit the beacon to raise the alarm! Shawe dragged her to the window and let out a curse. For that second his back was turned.

I had one brief chance to rescue Cat. I took it. I leapt across the room and flung myself at him. He staggered, unbalanced, banging his head hard on the window. As he reeled, his sword clattered to the floor. Cat wrenched herself from his grasp, spun round and jabbed him hard in the belly with her fist. Caught off-guard, he let out a yelp, doubled up in pain and crashed to the floor. I jumped onto his shoulders, hoping my feeble weight would hold him down. I was wrong! He raised himself, trying to shake me off.

I couldn't let him get free. I grabbed his hair and pulled hard. He roared with pain as his head was forced back, but he managed to stagger to his feet. Now I had my hands round his throat, but his fingers clamped my wrists as tight as a dog's jaws in a fight. He flung me aside and darted for his sword. I was helpless.

All I could focus on was the sword reflecting the firelight as it flashed towards me. But suddenly he gave a cry. He buckled where he stood and lay writhing on the floor, clutching his leg. I could see a dark stain oozing between his fingers.

Cat plonked herself determinedly on the prisoner's legs.

'Break my neck, would you?' she muttered, waving her scissors in his face. 'These points can do more damage than that!'

'You miserable little worms!' hissed Shawe, trying to squirm free.

'Don't kill him, Cat!' I yelled, wrenching his hands up behind his back. 'We need him alive.'

'I'm not going to kill him.' Cat grabbed the edge of her apron and began to cut it into long strips. 'Here . . .'

she tossed them over to me. 'Stop gawping and shut him up!'

I pulled his flailing arms together and between us we bound his wrists and ankles.

'You'll regret this!' yelled Shawe. 'You . . .' His words were muffled as I gagged him.

Cat jumped up and ran to the window. 'I don't think so,' she said. 'You'll be the one to regret what you've done. I can see a line of torches. The guards are on their way. Jack, we've won! . . . Jack?'

I couldn't share Cat's excitement. There was no triumph for me. I slumped down next to Aycliffe's body. I'd made a terrible mistake – a mistake that had cost a man his life. I felt nothing but utter despair seeing his lifeless body. I knew I was no longer worthy to be given special work by Master Cromwell. If I couldn't tell a friend from a foe he'd never trust me again.

Something stirred at the edge of my vision. I felt even worse. In my grief, I was imagining that Aycliffe's hand had moved. Wait! I was sure his finger had twitched. Then I heard a weak voice.

'Are you just going to sit there while I bleed to death?'

Robert Aycliffe's eyelids flickered. He was alive!

29

The next morning, Cat and I stood outside the golden doors of the King's Privy Apartments.

We were flanked by two unsmiling guards. I stifled a yawn. I'd been up most of the night telling Cromwell about Shawe's capture and now I wanted to hide in a corner and sleep. Cat grinned at me.

'Better not go yawning your head off when we're in front of His Majesty!' she whispered. 'By the way, why exactly have *I* been summoned to see him? You didn't tell Master Cromwell that I was there, did you? I mean, I know you'll always need my help, but I think of myself more as a sort of mysterious, shadowy figure in the background.'

I wanted to laugh at the thought of Cat as a mysterious, shadowy figure.

'I had to tell him everything that happened last night,' I replied. 'He couldn't complain. After all, you'd helped to catch a traitor. And anyway, Aycliffe and Shawe both saw what you did!'

'Don't utter my name with that villain's,' came a weak voice.

We turned to see Robert Aycliffe walking slowly up to us, holding his side and leaning awkwardly on a stick. He eased himself down onto a bench. He looked as pale as one of Cat's ghosts.

'Have you been summoned too?' I asked in surprise. 'Surely His Majesty can't have been told of your injuries or he would have left you to recover.'

'When the King commands, we all obey without question,' said Aycliffe. 'In any case, I am not so badly hurt as it might seem. As the traitor's blade struck I managed to turn away so it only cut through my flesh.'

'But you looked so . . . dead!' exclaimed Cat. 'That was clever.'

'Not really,' admitted Aycliffe. 'The sword may not have hit anything vital but the pain was too much to bear. I passed out.' He waved a hand. 'But enough of this. Before we are called in, I want to thank you both properly for what you did last night.'

'It was nothing, sir,' said Cat breezily. 'Always happy to be of assistance.'

I didn't speak. A lead weight seemed to be pressing down on me. Aycliffe looked at me. 'You're troubled, Jack. You should be proud of your actions.'

'But I mistook you for the traitor!' The words came

out in a rush. 'It could have been a fatal mistake. It almost was.'

Aycliffe smiled at me. 'You mustn't worry about that,' he said. 'Francis Shawe was very convincing, curse him. He had me fooled for many months – even last night when he left me a message that he'd discovered who the traitor was and wanted my help to trap him at Duke Humphrey's tower. It was only when he drew his sword on me that I discovered the truth.'

'I'll never doubt you again,' I told him earnestly.

'Doubt everyone, Jack,' said Aycliffe, his face solemn now. 'Besides, you're a better agent for Cromwell than I am. I let friendship blind me. You put King Henry and England first.'

This was praise but I wasn't sure I wanted it. I'd agreed to work for Master Cromwell and I knew I should do whatever it took. But did I want to be ruthless and cold-blooded? Perhaps I had no choice.

'And you caused quite a stir, I hear, Miss Thimblebee,' said Aycliffe.

'What do you mean?' demanded Cat.

'Your beacon set off a chain of beacons,' he laughed. 'They'd been lit as far as Highgate Hill before a messenger on a fast horse was able to quash the fear of invasion.'

'Lord have mercy!' gasped Cat.

The doors swung open and one of the King's Gentlemen appeared.

'His Majesty awaits!' he announced.

Aycliffe got slowly to his feet. I offered him my arm and we followed the messenger through one chamber and then another. Cat trotted along behind, gawping at the splendid objects all around us. Wax candles burned everywhere, lighting up gold clocks, jewelled chalices and the rich tapestries of mermaids and ugly sea gods on the wall. We walked on a long narrow carpet covered in red Tudor roses.

'I'm scared I'll make it dirty,' whispered Cat, her eyes on the deep wool under her feet.

At last we came to two heavy carved doors. The guards there stood aside and we were shown into the Privy Chamber.

Cromwell stood in the centre of the room, talking with other courtiers in their finest clothes, with gold chains round their necks. They looked towards us as we entered and acknowledged Robert Aycliffe with a friendly nod. They ignored me and Cat. We were obviously beneath their notice.

At the far end of the room was a throne under a canopy of rich silk hangings.

A door to one side opened and we all bowed deeply as the King entered.

'We have grave business in hand,' he said, taking his seat. 'Fetch the traitor.'

The order was given and Shawe was dragged in. His hands were manacled and his arms were in the grip of two yeomen guards. They pushed him into a kneeling position at the King's feet. He turned a mocking gaze on Aycliffe.

'I can hardly stand to look on you, sirrah!' snarled King Henry. 'There is no greater crime than treason. What do you have to say for yourself?'

Shawe's head flew up. 'You imbeciles should be bowing to me!' he declared, with a look of wild defiance. 'I fooled each one of you.'

'You dare to put yourself above us all!' thundered the King. Then he gave a grim smile. 'You're not the man you think you are. It only took two young ghost hunters to overcome you.'

Cromwell stepped forwards. 'Tell us about your Spanish masters, Francis,' he said quietly. 'It will go better for you if you don't have to be . . . persuaded.'

'I believe I am quite safe from the torturer's attentions,' said Shawe, a sly look on his face. 'I can prove most valuable to you. I will pretend to continue my work for King Charles in Toledo but I will in fact be loyal to England. I will be the best spy you've ever had. After all, only I was able to find the hidden passages here in Greenwich Palace and use them to my advantage.'

'Passages!' gasped one of the courtiers. 'What is he talking about?'

The King looked furious.

Shawe didn't seem to notice. 'You would be foolish not to take me up on my offer,' he carried on smoothly. 'Think what benefits you will gain by having me on your side. Give me a royal pardon, Sire, and together we can bring down Spain.'

'You have a black heart and know not what loyalty is, Francis Shawe.' The King spoke so quietly that we all craned forwards to hear his words. 'You have betrayed us once. You would do so again.'

'I believe you will soon be singing about Spain at the top of your voice,' added Cromwell darkly. 'Whether you choose to or not.'

I saw Cat shudder at the thought of what awaited Shawe. We both knew it would be a fate far worse than anything he had inflicted on poor Miles Hawkesworth.

And at last Shawe understood too. He turned deathly pale. 'Forgive me, my noble Liege,' he cried brokenly as he grovelled at the King's feet. 'In truth I was forced into this dreadful work by the Spanish. I have ever been mindful of protecting the life of my sovercign. I found out about the hidden passages from an old map. Remember that with this knowledge I could have killed you as you slept . . .'

'Silence!' The room itself seemed to shake at His Majesty's roar. 'You are a traitor and a murderer. The body of Miles Hawkesworth has been recovered. You gave him no mercy.' King Henry turned his gaze on the guards. 'Take this treacherous cur from my sight.'

The guards seized Shawe. He gazed wildly round the wall of grim faces as if seeking help from somewhere. Then his eyes met mine in a sudden look of understanding that sent ice through my blood.

'Ghost hunter?' He spat at my feet. 'No. I see now what you really are.' My heart began to race. Shawe was going to have his revenge. He was going to expose me and there was nothing I could do about it.

30

'Why is this villain still in my sight?' roared King Henry, cutting across Shawe's words.

The yeomen did not need telling twice. Before he could reveal anything else, Shawe was dragged across the floor and out of the chamber.

The rage gone as quickly as it had come, His Majesty calmly put his hand on my shoulder. 'It seems that our traitor did not want to believe he was beaten by a mere scribe and seamstress out searching for ghosts,' he told the assembled ministers.

'With one so vain as Shawe,' added Cromwell, 'that would be humiliation indeed!'

The courtiers all laughed.

'Shawe has lost his wits with fear,' I heard one whisper to his neighbour.

'Everyone to his business,' commanded the King. 'There is much to be done. The passages that the perfidious rat spoke of must be filled in. I have a new song to write – one not tainted by that traitor. And this afternoon we will bury Mister Hawkesworth in the churchyard. Then we will feast in his honour.'

Cat and I stood back while the ministers and Aycliffe took their leave. We were about to follow in their wake when the King called us back. Cat and I went down on our knees in front of him.

'Master Cromwell has told me all about your *ghost hunting*,' he said. 'And I feel such enterprise should have some reward. Tell me what you would like. Although I'd heard you came into some money, Jack Briars.'

I looked up, expecting to see an angry expression on his face. After all, I'd only got the winnings because of his ill temper! But his eyes were twinkling. I thought ruefully of my lost coins as the King went on. 'I can think of something that you might find useful. When Aycliffe is fully recovered, he will instruct you in the art of sword fighting. You never know when you might need it.'

'Thank you, Sire,' I gasped. 'That would be wonderful.'

He turned to Cat. 'And what would you like?'

'Well, my Liege,' said Cat, her voice hushed in awe. 'I did have to cut up a perfectly good apron to restrain Mister Shawe.'

'Then you must have a new one. And a new dress as well.'

'Thank you, my Liege. That will be perfect, my Liege. I'm ever so grateful, my Liege!'

He waved us away and, after making our bows, we were led out of the royal apartments.

'I forgot to give you this.' Cat pressed some coins into my hand – ten silver sixpences.

'How . . . ?' I began.

She shrugged. 'Oswyn's purse and my scissors had a small accident.'

'Poor Oswyn,' I said, grinning. 'Thanks, Cat. I'll buy you something. What would you like?'

'Red ribbons,' said Cat promptly. 'No, a new cap for my new dress . . . or some marchpane shaped like . . .'

Luckily Cromwell joined us at that moment.

'Walk with me, Jack,' he said. His tone was neutral and I couldn't guess at his mood. But I knew a command when I heard one.

We set off. I noticed Cat was following, keeping her distance. But I'd wager all my winnings that she was close enough to hear.

'Well, Jack,' said Cromwell. 'I join the King in commending you for your actions.'

'I was merely following orders, sir,' I said.

Cromwell raised an eyebrow. 'And going beyond them. I don't recall telling you to deliver the traitor to me.'

'No, sir,' I replied, 'but when you go ghost hunting, you never know what's going to happen.'

I wasn't sure whether I'd gone too far, but Cromwell

merely smiled. 'I was not wrong when I recruited you, Jack. You've proved yourself up to any task I throw at you and there will be more, I can promise you that. Well done. You have done great service for your country.' He looked over his shoulder. 'You both have!'

I thought Cat would be abashed but she just grinned from ear to ear and made him a bow. Chuckling, Cromwell headed off.

I watched him go, a warm feeling in my chest.

Cat caught me up.

'He's a good man,' she said. 'Not too high and mighty to give praise to a lowly seamstress.'

'He was praising me too,' I told her. 'And it was my mission, don't forget.'

'You couldn't have done it without me!' insisted Cat. 'Me and my scissors!'

She was right! And she'd had the last word as usual. But this time I didn't care. It was enough that Master Cromwell believed in me. There would be plenty more secret tasks coming my way. Let them come!